Seven Birthday Wishes

MELISSA SENATE

D0037243

HARLEQUIN
**SPECIAL
EDITION**

HARLEQUIN®
SPECIAL
EDITION™

Recycling programs
for this product may
not exist in your area.

ISBN-13: 978-1-335-72474-8

Seven Birthday Wishes

Harlequin Enterprises ULC
22 Adelaide St. West, 41st Floor
Toronto, Ontario M5H 4E3, Canada
www.Harlequin.com

Printed in U.S.A.

Melissa Senate has written many novels for Harlequin and other publishers, including her debut, *See Jane Date*, which was made into a TV movie. She also wrote seven books for Harlequin Special Edition under the pen name Meg Maxwell. Her novels have been published in over twenty-five countries. Melissa lives on the coast of Maine with her teenage son; their rescue shepherd mix, Flash; and a lap cat named Cleo. For more information, please visit her website, melissasenate.com.

For my beloved son.

Chapter One

"Guess what, Mommy?" seven-year-old Cody Dawson called as he leaped off the school bus in front of the gates to the Dawson Family Guest Ranch. "You'll never guess, that's what!"

Annabel Dawson smiled at her son and waved at the bus driver, who turned the big yellow rig around and headed back up the long drive. 3:38 p.m. was her favorite time of day—when she met Cody at the gates and they walked the quarter mile to their cabin. One of the perks of working at her cousin's dude ranch was that it was so family-friendly; Annabel's hours as a wilderness tour guide for guests were structured around Cody's school day. She didn't work nights or weekends. A single mother, Annabel was grateful for her six cousins who owned the ranch and had welcomed her with a job, a cozy cabin and subsidized on-site day care when Cody was six months old.

"Hmm, you got a hundred on your spelling test?" she asked, leaning down to give Cody a hug.

"Actually, I got two wrong," he said. "But no, that's not it!" He jumped up and down in excitement, his mop of light brown hair flopping in the early-June breeze. "Guess again!"

"Someone traded you their chocolate chip cookies for your red grapes at lunch?" she tried.

"Mommy, be serious! Who would do that?"

She laughed. "Your loose tooth came out? Should I expect the tooth fairy to visit tonight while you're sleeping?"

A finger went to the wobbly bottom tooth. "Nope, still there! Guess again!"

"Hmm, I think you're just gonna have to tell me the big news," she said as they headed through the ornate wrought iron gates of the ranch. "I'm all out of guesses."

"Okay, I will!" he said, his bright smile and utter happiness making her day—and she'd had a rough start.

A little girl on one of her group tours in the woods had refused to take another step or listen to her parents, who'd tried to coax her into moving with offers of a brownie from the ranch's cafeteria. That didn't work and the girl ran off the path into the brush, crying that she was getting scratched by leafy branches. The father chased after her, came out with the girl sobbing in his arms, and Annabel heard later that both daughter and father had gotten poison ivy. Annabel had visited their cabin not fifteen minutes ago with a "treat" basket that the guest relations manager, her cousin Daisy, had helped her create. The Selman family, including the mother, who'd been holding a tube of calamine lotion when she opened the door, looked positively miserable. And then on a late-morning tour, a teenager had screamed, "Grizzly!" and pointed toward the woods, and everyone had freaked out, despite the teen bursting into laughter and doubling over a second later. Yeah, real funny. Yup, it had been that kind of day.

"The *best* thing happened at school!" Cody said, grabbing her hand and pulling her to a bench across from the Welcome Hut. After shrugging out of his backpack, he dropped it on the bench and rummaged through it to pull out his blue take-home folder. "Look in there!" he said, jumping up and down and spinning around.

Wow. This *had* to be good. Maybe there was a special event planned for the end of the school year? An exciting field trip or color war before summer break in three weeks?

She opened the folder and looked through it. There was his reading log, then a permission slip to a field trip to this very ranch's petting zoo during the last week of school and then a returned homework assignment: My Hero. There was a gold star at the top and a note from his teacher attached to it.

Annabel inwardly sighed, a little lump forming in her throat as one had every time she'd dealt with this assignment. *My hero is Logan Winston*, the essay began, Cody's careful handwriting in pencil taking up just six lines.

When Cody had come home with the assignment in his folder last week, she'd instantly known he'd write about Logan. She'd barely gotten through her son thinking out loud as he'd decided what he wanted to say in his essay. And for a second grader, each sentence took a lot of thinking, a lot of time, a lot of consulting his spelling lists. When she'd read the finished essay, the sweetness—and her secret—hit her hard.

Logan Winston had been her son's hero for a couple of years now, ever since her father had taken his grandson on a surprise trip to the rodeo. The champion bull rider with the trademark black Stetson with its studded silver leather band had legions of fans of all ages.

Annabel wasn't one of them. She used to be, though. Way before he'd ever won a competition.

If she'd known her dad was going to take Cody to his first rodeo when the state championships were held a few towns over, she probably would have come up with some excuse why they shouldn't go. Ever since, Cody mentioned Logan Winston at least once a day. His old rodeo tickets were all neatly pinned on the corkboard above his desk. He had a Logan Winston lunch box. A Logan Winston T-shirt. A Logan Winston poster on his bedroom wall—which Annabel was always careful not to look at.

Logan Winston was Cody's father. And Annabel was the only person in the world who knew.

I hope I get to meet Logan Winston someday, Cody had said a bunch of times the past two years while she'd tuck him in, his gaze dreamy on the poster. It was especially then that Annabel's own eyes would start stinging with tears. Her son's hero was the father he also asked about more and more these days.

What do you think my daddy is doing right now? Cody had asked two nights ago during his bubble bath, dueling cowboy figurines in his hands.

Living his dream, she'd think, unsure, as always, if she'd done the right thing by never informing Logan he had a child.

If he knew about you, he'd be thinking about you right now, she'd said to Cody, and he seemed satisfied with that. She'd told her son the basic truth—that she hadn't known she was pregnant with him when his father had left town and she hadn't known how to reach him.

But that had only been true till the end of her pregnancy, when Logan Winston had started making a name for himself. She'd been eighteen years old, nine months pregnant, her parents supportive but doing a lot of deep sighing, when she'd seen Logan's face on the front page of the *Bear Ridge Free Weekly*—Hometown Bull Rider Is Now 10-0! Every day she'd think about trying to get in touch. But she'd always come back to what he'd said the night before he'd left.

I never want kids. Ever.

"Mommy, I'll bet Logan Winston sees my essay on the front page of the newspaper tomorrow!" Cody said excitedly. He spun around and then crouched down as if on the back of a bull, one hand on the rope, the other in the air, like his hero.

Wait, what? Front page? That was when Annabel actually read the note attached to the returned essay from Cody's teacher, Ms. Gattano.

Hi Annabel! Exciting news! I sent the kids' essays to the Wyoming Gazette and not only are they printing photos of all fourteen kids holding up their essays in the People and Community page tomorrow, but they've chosen to feature Cody's photo and essay on the front page tomorrow alongside an article about Logan Winston. Wow! Cody is so excited! Don't miss the paper tomorrow!—Ms. G.

Annabel's hand flew to her mouth. Oh God. Oh boy. Oh whoa.

The *Wyoming Gazette* was a major daily newspaper. Everyone had a *Wyoming Gazette* delivery box next to their mailbox. Everyone read the *Gazette*.

Her heart started hammering.

"I know, Mommy!" Cody said, jumping up and down again. "My hero is gonna see my essay for sure!"

Would he? She bit her lip. She highly doubted Logan Winston read his own press anymore. This kind of feature in the *Gazette* had to be everyday stuff for him. He certainly hadn't seemed interested in the news, local or otherwise, when they'd dated those three short days. He'd seemed only interested in her, bull riding and working as a cowboy at the Sattler Ranch, a huge operation where there was always overtime, so he could pay for practice time.

He had to be way too busy these days. Annabel had long stopped following his career; she only had in the beginning, six, seven years ago because she'd been so proud of him. Hurt, yes, but proud nonetheless. He'd done it. Dreams he could barely mention aloud because they seemed so far-fetched to him had actually come true—and then some. Almost eight years ago, as a beginner, he'd never lasted the eight seconds on the back of a bull. But when he left Bear Ridge—and her—he'd started placing in competitions. Within a year, she'd seen another article about him in the county-wide newspaper: Local Bull Rider Wins Big at the Bear County Rodeo.

Within two years, he was on the front page of the

Wyoming Gazette—and often. And these days, he was a superstar, a champion no one could touch in the arena in terms of control, command and style. Add in his good looks and Logan Winston was a town, state and western regional hero whose events sold out far in advance.

Even if he did see the front page of the *Gazette*, even if he did read the essay by a little kid who hero-worshipped him, he wouldn't necessarily connect the last name with the girl he'd known for three days almost eight years ago.

The girl he'd unknowingly left pregnant.

Bear Ridge was full of Dawsons, and Cody Dawson could be any of their sons.

Logan Winston, superstar bull rider, would not connect the dots. Or likely even notice them in the first place.

As they approached their cabin, which was nestled into a stand of trees across the wide path from the petting zoo, Annabel could see her mom sitting on the porch swing. Dinah Dawson's face was lifted to the bright summer sunshine, silvery-blond bob gleaming.

Oh, thank God, Annabel thought. Her mom sometimes surprised them with a visit after school. If there was anyone she needed to talk to right now, it was Dinah Dawson.

"Grammy, guess what?" Cody called out when he noticed her, running ahead up the steps.

"What?" Dinah asked, popping up to wrap her

grandson in a big hug and give him a loud smooch on his head. There was a telltale white bag beside the porch swing with the gold Bear Ridge Bakery logo on it.

"My homework essay about my hero is going to be in the newspaper!" Cody announced.

"Wow!" Dinah said. "How exciting! I don't have to guess who your hero is. Logan Winston, am I right?"

Cody gave a big nod. "He's the GOAT of bull riders! That means greatest of all time, Grammy."

Grammy grinned and ruffled Cody's hair. "And *you* are the GOAT of grandsons!"

Cody giggled and ran inside the cabin, her mom picking up the bakery bag and following him. Annabel took a deep breath and headed in. Cody rushed for the laptop on the desk in the living room. "Mommy, can I watch the video of Logan's wins?"

"Sure," she called. He'd only watched it fifty times since his grandfather had shot it from the stands at the last rodeo they'd gone to. Her dad was gone now; they'd lost him just seven months after that rodeo. Every time Cody watched it, it was her dad who Annabel thought of, her dad who had the grip of her memories. Somehow, that made it bittersweet instead of downright difficult when the announcer would give his second-by-second account of Logan's every move, from his expression to his free hand to the one on the rope.

Her mom followed her into the kitchen and beelined for the coffee maker. She held up the bakery bag and opened it, showing Annabel the goodies inside—her favorite tart—chocolate cream—a mixed-berry scone for Annabel and a peanut butter cookie for Cody. Annabel grabbed a string cheese from the fridge and a clementine and brought the snack over to Cody, who was entranced by the video.

Oh God, oh God, oh God, she thought, her knees suddenly shaking. She hurried back into the kitchen and dropped down on a chair at the table.

"Annabel? You okay?" her mom asked, tilting her head and looking at her. "You look kind of…sickish."

"I'm not really okay," she whispered. She let out a breath and bit her lip and looked everywhere but her mother's face. "I mean, I'm okay, Cody's okay. Something's just…come up."

Her mother's eyes widened. "Oooh boy, let's sit down with our coffee and goodies and you'll tell me everything."

Annabel nodded but she wasn't sure she *would* tell. How did you just blurt out something so…big after seven years?

Her mother poured two coffees and fixed them up, plopped the treats on a plate, and sat down beside Annabel, whose legs were still shaking. She popped up and grabbed Cody's backpack from the hook beside the front door, taking a peek at him as she went back into the kitchen. He'd restarted the video, which her dad had mixed with others of Logan's competitions. He'd be set for a bit.

"Okay," Annabel said, sitting back down with the folder. She took out the essay and pointed at the note from the teacher.

Her mom read it, then looked at Annabel. "But that's great! So what's wrong?"

Annabel shook her head. She closed her eyes for a second.

"Annabel, honeybun, what's going on?" Dinah whispered, scooting her chair a little closer. She strained her neck to see into the living room, as did Annabel. Cody was still entranced by the video and she had no doubt he'd watch it again.

Was she just going to come out with it? Say the words out loud after keeping the secret all these years? Her mouth was dry. She took a fast sip of her coffee, then a deep breath.

She'd never forget the day she discovered she was pregnant. She'd been taking two classes at the local college in animal husbandry and agriculture while working at a nearby ranch and she realized her period was really late. It never was. So she'd bought a home pregnancy test—she'd driven to the next town because everyone in Bear Ridge knew one another. She'd taken the test, following the directions to a tee, expecting not to see an orange plus sign appear in the second window.

It appeared.

She'd been shocked and took the second test in the box.

For an hour she'd hidden in her room, scared, crying, a mess. And when her mom called her down to help with dinner prep, she'd blurted out the news.

Dinah had pulled her eighteen-year-old daughter into an embrace, told her everything would be okay, then had asked who the father was. Tears streaming down her face, Annabel had told the truth: that he was someone she'd had a *very* brief romance with but he'd left town. She didn't mention his name; Logan had been a few years older and had a reputation for getting into trouble with the law.

You call him right this minute, Dinah had said. *Let him know you have something important to tell him.*

Annabel had pulled out her phone. She'd pressed in the numbers. Then panicked and clicked End Call. That had gone on for a full minute.

She'd told her mom how one of the last things he'd said to her was that he didn't want kids ever. *No responsibilities, no ties, no way to disappoint anyone who'd count on me.*

Dinah had raised an eyebrow. *The guy is the father of your baby whether he wants to be or not.*

Annabel had ignored the ache in her chest. The raw, burning strain in her throat. And made the call.

The number you have reached is a nonworking number...

She'd tried it again. And a third time, just in case she'd entered it wrong out of nerves.

The number you have reached...

She'd been so shocked, so...hurt, that she'd just handed the phone to her mother and sobbed. He'd been gone six weeks by then and clearly had cut all ties to Bear Ridge if he'd disconnected his cell phone.

Well, maybe he'll come back, her mother had said, biting her lip.

Now Annabel looked at the teacher's note again. She took another sip of coffee.

Say it. Tell her.

Annabel tapped the essay—right next to the first line. *My hero is Logan Winston...* "Logan Winston is Cody's father," she whispered.

Her mother gasped, then slapped her hand over mouth, leaning back to strain her neck to make sure Cody was occupied. "No," she said in disbelief.

Annabel nodded.

She whispered the short story of their romance, gulping down some more coffee, her appetite gone for the scone. How the night before he'd left, they'd taken a picnic to Clover Mountain and she'd felt so madly in love. He'd surprised her by taking her to a B and B in the more bustling town twenty minutes away, which back then had required telling her mom a fib about where she was spending the night. Then he'd gotten a phone call that had poured cold water on him for a little while, Logan seeming agitated and disgruntled but refusing to talk about it. He'd gone onto their balcony and stared up at the stars for a few minutes, and had apologized and said he was damned lucky to be here with her and she was all that mattered. But as they'd talked about their hopes and dreams, and she'd mentioned she wanted a big family someday, four or five kids because she was an only, he'd blurted out what he had about kids. About ties and how he didn't want them. In the morning he'd texted her that he was sorry, he really liked her, but he had to get out of Bear Ridge, that the town was killing him and he'd just end up in jail or dead if he stayed.

"Six weeks later," Annabel said, "I was late and finally took a home pregnancy test. You know the rest now."

"Oh, Annabel." Her mom leaned over to pull her into a hug.

The embrace felt so good. Dinah had been full of extra hugs ever since the day Annabel had revealed her pregnancy. Her mother had told her father, who'd then knocked on Annabel's door and just hugged her and said that everything would be okay, not necessarily easy anymore, but okay. *Wonderful, even*, he'd added. She missed her dad so much.

"So when you could get in touch with Logan, you just…couldn't?" her mom asked.

Annabel nodded. "I kept remembering what he'd said about not wanting kids, how he'd changed his number. How his dreams were all coming true. So I kept my secret. He never came back to Bear Ridge, as far as I know. Even when his father died last year. And I watched him become a bigger and bigger celebrity to the point that he stopped seeming real, you know?"

"He didn't come home for his father's funeral?" her mother asked. "I think I'd read somewhere that his mother died when he was ten years old?"

Annabel nodded. "I guess his father was part of the problems he had in Bear Ridge. Must have been big for him not to go to his funeral. He'd told me that he and his father had never gotten along, but he didn't elaborate. I remember him telling me how lucky I was that I was close to my parents."

Dinah reached over to squeeze Annabel's hand. "It must have been so hard when Cody started hero-worshipping him."

Annabel nodded. "I felt terrible. I was bursting with the truth. So many times I almost broke down to tell you, Mom. But I'd get gripped by fear, that too much time had passed, that people would think I was coming forward because Logan was famous. I know that's cowardly, but I was just so scared. And now it's been almost eight years."

Her mom drained the rest of her coffee. "Well, just like I said when you told me you were pregnant, he *is* the father. He should know about Cody. And Cody should know about him. This whole thing with the essay and the *Wyoming Gazette*? It's the universe's way of telling you it's time."

Annabel could barely breathe.

It *was* time.

Chapter Two

Logan Winston was having one heck of a bad day. A bad couple of days.

He was slouched in the passenger seat of his manager's Range Rover, trying not to look at the thing on his wrist—a black brace placed there five minutes ago by his orthopedist. How many times had Savannah Walsh told him he should be grateful the injury wasn't worse? Twice in the last five minutes alone. A hundred times since yesterday.

He actually *was* grateful. Grumpy but grateful. He scowled at the brace, then looked out the window at the passing scenery in Blue Smoke, Wyoming. As they neared Burger Delight, his favorite take-out joint, he had a craving for their curly fries with spicy ranch sauce. And a Sprite.

"Pull into the drive-through, Savannah," he said, upping his chin. "I need fries."

He could feel his manager's hawklike eyes narrowed on him. "Logan, have you been listening to a word I've said since we left Dr. Russo's office?" she barked.

The streaming commentary on everything the ER doctor had said yesterday and which his long-standing orthopedist had repeated ten minutes ago? No, he hadn't been listening. He'd heard it all twice already. Sprained ligament. One week rest. No lifting anything heavier than a tissue with his injured wrist.

All because yesterday at the practice pen, Bulliminator, one of the roughest rides, had almost bested him, Logan coming close to being flung off the bull's back. A rarity. Righting himself had done in his wrist.

"And what you *need*," Savannah continued, "is a high-protein, high-fiber smoothie for muscle and tissue recovery. Not those greasy fries you love so much. We'll stop at Smoothie Smash for a white bean and flaxseed concoction—that's my order lately and now I'm running an extra mile every morning."

He grimaced at just the thought of that smoothie. "I'll take the fries. And no, I haven't been listening. I'm trying to *forget* the injury for the fifteen-minute drive home, not focus on it."

Now it was Savannah's turn to sigh. She turned into the Burger Delight lot, following the sign for the drive-through. As they waited behind four cars, she turned to him. "Logan, look at me for two seconds. Please."

He sat up and turned toward her, tilting his Stetson up on his head. Savannah deserved his respect. She'd been his manager for seven years and was invaluable, worth every cent of the small fortune he paid her. Tall and slender, with a shock of red hair to her chin, a swish of bangs and constantly assessing brown eyes behind round crystal-framed glasses, Savannah was only five years older than he was, but light years ahead of him in just about every regard.

"You're lucky the state championships in Cheyenne is three days *past* your prescribed one-week rest period, Logan. What's not so lucky? That you can't *practice*."

He hated the whole thing, but he especially hated that part. Logan hadn't skipped a day of practice since he won his first competition—when he discovered he might have it in him after all to be a champion bull rider.

Savannah pushed her glasses up on her nose. "The rodeo in Cheyenne is a huge deal, and you want to walk away with the quarter million. But more importantly, you want to defend your status as reigning state champ. These two just under you, Brandon Lopez and Dallas Parker—they're salivating that you're nursing an injury. And so are the media—you know how many calls and texts and emails I got from reporters two minutes after your injury? Ten before you even arrived at the ER. Word spreads fast, Logan. Everyone is watching this. You need to rest up that wrist. A true recuperation. Then you'll practice—practice *light*—for the two days before the rodeo."

"I'll rest up," he assured her. That he *would* do. Bull riding was his life.

"And I have just the place for that," she added, taking a folded newspaper out of the tote bag at her side and resting it on the console between them. Today's *Wyoming Gazette*. He glanced at it. On the front page was a story about his injury—and next to it, a photo of a kid wearing one of his promo T-shirts and holding up a piece of paper with both hands and a huge smile on his face. He was missing two teeth. Logan peered closer at the sheet of paper. It was titled My Hero.

He slouched back down and looked out the window. Yesterday, before practice, before Bulliminator, he'd been mobbed by kids on a field trip to the arena, signing what seemed like hundreds of autographs. Logan always gave 100 percent to his young fans. But here in the sanctuary of the Range Rover with its tinted windows, he preferred a kid-free zone.

The car ahead moved up and Savannah inched forward in the drive-through. "That cute boy in the photo is holding up the essay he wrote about you for a homework assignment on their heroes. He's from Bear Ridge, our mutual hometown."

Even almost eight years after leaving Bear Ridge, hearing the name of the small town still sent up a chill up his spine. Savannah never mentioned any-thing unless there was an *and* to come. Did he want to hear whatever it was? Probably not.

"This piece on you in today's *Gazette* was sup-posed to be about your one hundred percent odds of winning Cheyenne. But instead it's about your in-jury and how you might not be able to defend your title, let alone keep it. We need a good spin for your recuperation. And this kid is it," she added, jabbing a finger at the boy in the photo.

That was a big *and*. "Not sure I want to hear this, Savannah."

She moved the SUV forward. They were one car away from ordering. "You'll recuperate in Bear Ridge for the week," Savannah said. "At the dude ranch where your number one fan, little Cody Dawson, lives. The Dawson Family Guest Ranch—"

Logan sat up straight and grabbed the newspaper. Cody *Dawson*?

Maybe related to Annabel Dawson? A nephew? No, wait, Annabel was an only child. Maybe Cody was a cousin. Bear Ridge was full of Dawsons.

Or maybe she'd gotten married and had a child.

He felt a strange squeeze in his chest at just the thought. Despite not having seen Annabel Dawson in almost eight years. And they'd only known each other for three days.

Logan looked at the photo of the kid and read the caption: *Seven-year-old Cody Dawson, Logan Winston's self-proclaimed number one fan!* The boy held up the essay, which had a gold star sticker at the top. He had light brown hair and hazel eyes. He looked like Annabel, even though she was very blonde with eyes the color of driftwood.

Logan read the short essay, in a boxed sidebar beside the boy's photo.

My Hero.

By Cody Dawson, Age 7, Bear Ridge, Wyoming.

My hero is Logan Winston. Logan Winston is a bull rider. He is the GOAT of bull riders. GOAT means Greatest of All Time.

Logan Winston is my hero because he is nice to bulls. He always talks to the bull while he holds on for the eight seconds. If I could meet my hero, I would ask him what he says.

Aww, that was cute. Logan did always talk to the bulls.

He glanced at the line with the name and age. Seven. If Annabel Dawson *was* Cody's mother, she must have gotten married right after he left. For a good six months, he used to imagine her sitting out on the flat expanse of roof by her bedroom window, staring up at the stars—and thinking about him. Wishing him well, even if he'd very abruptly ended their short but good thing. But she obviously hadn't been. She'd gotten over him fast, not that he blamed her, and found someone else. He'd been trouble back then—pissed off, a loner, surely headed down the same road to nowhere as his father.

He'd gotten into a bad argument with his dad just before he'd come across Annabel standing beside a hissing beater car on a remote road on a cold March day. Logan had recognized her from his high school, though she was a few years younger. He was twenty-one then, she just eighteen. She'd always stood out to him and she had that day, even in baggy overalls and a puffy silver coat, a long blond ponytail snaking down her back from the Quarry Ranch cap she wore. He'd waited with her until the tow truck came, then offered to drive her home, which led to her thanking him with pizza at his favorite place. Then a walk in the flurries coming down in the park before talking about everything and anything and stealing glances at each other to his small cabin on the ranch where he worked. They'd spent three days together, and he'd almost forgotten everything that bothered him about his life. Almost.

Most good things didn't last anyway. Except his career, which was why he'd forced himself to listen to Savannah and do what she said. She'd never steered him wrong, not since he was twenty-one and "showed promise she last saw with Toby Diggon," who'd been one of his bull-riding heroes. That he and Savannah were both from the same hometown had kind of bonded them initially, even though they hadn't known each other growing up and she liked the place and he didn't. He'd said yes to her managing him and it was the second decision he'd never questioned. The first was putting everything he had into bull riding.

Had it not been for Annabel and having to leave her behind, getting the hell out of Bear Ridge would have been first on his list of good decisions. He'd fallen for her hard. Even at just eighteen, she'd known who she was and what she wanted, which was life as a cowgirl, her own ranch and for those three days—him. But he'd gotten into the last big fight with his father he ever would—a promise to himself—and he'd left town the next morning with a short text to Annabel saying he was sorry, that he liked her a lot but he had to leave. He'd cut ties with his hometown, with his father, with his past—and canceled his cell phone service. A new number, a new ranch job that came with room and board, and no one from his past could find him. Unreachable— that was what he'd needed to be.

He'd had to end a promising new relationship. And Annabel had been special. But what relationship of his had ever worked out anyway?

Besides, she'd said she wanted a big family some-day—four or five children since she was an only—

and he didn't want *any*. Even though he, too, was an only. He'd told her that, too.

"You know this kid or something?" Savannah asked, breaking into his memories.

Logan realized he was clutching the newspaper and staring hard at the photo of little Cody Dawson. He set it down on the console.

"I know someone with the last name," he said. "Lots of Dawsons in Bear Ridge, though. Might not be a relation—"

He froze as a thought—and some math—slammed into his head.

He and Annabel had been together *almost eight years ago*.

She and his number one fan had the same last name.

And the boy was *seven*.

But he and Annabel had used protection—every time during those three days. They'd gone through an entire box and had had to go to the drugstore to buy a new box. No way was Cody Dawson, age seven, *his*.

Though condoms could break, he supposed. But if he'd gotten Annabel pregnant, she would have contacted him a long time ago. Yeah, he'd canceled his cell phone service and left no forwarding address to cut all ties to his dad and Bear Ridge, but once he got well known in Bear County, she could have easily found him—if need be.

Cody Dawson, who liked that he talked to bulls,

couldn't be his son. It was just too unlikely, and the idea of Logan Winston as someone's father was downright unthinkable. He wasn't meant for a family. And he wouldn't know the first thing about being a dad.

Like he'd just said to Savannah, Bear Ridge was Dawson country. One branch of the family had six siblings and they probably all had kids by now. Cody Dawson was probably one of theirs.

"So here's the plan," Savannah said. "We'll snap some photos of you and the kid at the dude ranch. We'll interview him, get some great sound bites, and spin the social media posts to how resting your sprained wrist gives you this opportunity to surprise a young hometown fan who'll get to ask his hero what he says to the bulls." She grinned. "Folks'll eat it up, Logan. They'll be rooting for you to heal up and win big in Cheyenne."

He'd been so focused on his fan's last name that he hadn't zeroed in on the part about *staying* in Bear Ridge. That was a no. "Can't we do all that here in Blue Smoke at the training arena?" he asked. "We'll hire a limo to bring him and his parents here. I'm not stepping foot in Bear Ridge."

"Logan. You need to be in Bear Ridge for the reasons I stated. But there's one more. The big one. The one that got you injured yesterday."

That got his attention. "What big one?"

"Your past," she said, her brown eyes going from

shrewd to compassionate. "I know your father died a year ago—coming up on a year, actually, next week. You didn't go to the funeral—I know that, too, because I'm on top of your schedule. I do know you handled arrangements, but from afar. I also know you haven't been yourself since you heard he passed. You've been...distant. Off. Still winning big, yes, but off. And now a week away from the anniversary of his death, you sprain your wrist by almost falling off during a *practice* run?" She shook her head. "Whatever you need to put to rest in Bear Ridge has the reins right now. Not you. And that's very dangerous. In more ways than one."

He leaned his head back against the seat. He had nothing to say. First of all, he didn't even know what he thought of what Savannah had just launched at him. Second, she was probably right. He'd been edgy and unsettled this past year. He'd thought it actually helped in the arena. But now, with the anniversary of his father's death coming up, he'd been distracted to the point that he *had* gotten injured. But go to Bear Ridge? The thought sent another icy shiver up his spine, dropped dread in his throat, his gut.

There was nothing to put to rest in Bear Ridge. His father was gone. All that was left was the run-down shack-like house that Logan had grown up in and run from the first chance he could at eighteen when he'd gotten a live-in job as a cowboy miles from his father.

"Oh, and I should mention I've already gone ahead and booked you into the last available VIP cabin at the Dawson Family Guest Ranch for the next week," Savannah said fast. "It's very popular and looks gorgeous from the photos. Great reviews, too. And the VIP cabins come with a concierge who'll get you anything you need and want. All the white bean and flaxseed smoothies you can drink."

He sighed inwardly but was more focused on wondering if Annabel was related to the Dawsons who owned the guest ranch. When he left town, that ranch had been long-abandoned and in bad shape. But someone had clearly gotten it going again. Maybe even Annabel. Maybe she'd made her dream come true of owning her own spread, a dude ranch.

He did like the idea of seeing her again, even if she was married with kids now. She'd been the one bright spot in his life back then. He'd always felt being with her for those magical three days had helped give him the confidence to finally leave and chase his dreams.

He owed her an apology for walking away from her after an intense romance—and a thank-you for changing his life. And this was crazy but he believed, deep down, that Annabel Dawson had some kind of magical powers and just seeing her face again, hearing her voice, would help—help settle what had gotten him distracted and injured. Just like she'd helped eight years ago. Without even knowing it. Maybe without him knowing until much later.

Just being near Annabel could even heal his wrist faster.

Yes, he owed her an apology and a thank-you. And the boy, if he *was* her child, could meet his hero and get all the free T-shirts and Logan Winston lunch boxes he wanted. Pencils with his name, too.

But most of all, he needed to make sure that Cody Dawson *wasn't* his child. Logan was 99 percent sure he wasn't. But there was a possibility. And Logan didn't like to let possibilities peck away at his gut. You had a question, you got it answered.

"Okay," he said. "I'm in."

Savannah's dark eyes got huge behind her round crystal frames. "No argument?"

"There's a reason I pay you the big bucks," he said.

She smiled and patted his arm. "God, I love when you're reasonable. I'll pick you up tomorrow afternoon at one. Check-in is at four."

Bear Ridge. The thought of that place, his memories, almost made him lose his appetite, but it was finally their turn to order at Burger Delight. Thanks to his not giving Savannah a hard time over staying in Bear Ridge, she got him the large-size curly fries with extra spicy ranch dipping sauce. He popped a fry into his mouth—ahh, delicious—and fifteen minutes later, they were at the gates of his condo complex.

He nodded at the attendant, and then Savannah wound her way to his unit with its high rock walls for privacy. He liked living in Blue Smoke, a big tourist town with its own weekly rodeo, a great practice arena and wide-open spaces where he could ride his horse, Sand Dune, far out in the country, and not run into another person. Blue Smoke didn't remind him at all of Bear Ridge, which was three hours away. Another reason he was comfortable here.

As he headed inside his condo and went into his bedroom to pack—one-handed, he'd been reminded by Savannah with a finger jabbed toward his chest— he was struck by a memory. Of being in bed with Annabel Dawson that final night at a B and B, how beautiful she'd been lying naked next to him, her head on his chest, his hands stroking her silky hair, those soulful driftwood-brown eyes. Being with Annabel had felt like what all those love songs were about. Almost eight years later, and he was still waiting to feel like that again, but Savannah liked that he never got serious about any of his dates or girlfriends. Less distraction, she'd say.

With his good hand he tossed two folded button-down shirts fresh from the dry cleaner into the suitcase. He'd take a tux and a suit, just in case, and there was always a "just in case" with Savannah as a manager.

Yes, he'd dutifully do as his manager wanted, apologize to Annabel, *not* deal with his past, tell his number one fan what he said to the bulls, breathe easier knowing he wasn't a father, rest up and then win big in Cheyenne, which was all that mattered.

Chapter Three

The next day, at 3:38 p.m., Annabel waited for the bus, which she could hear coming down the long drive to the ranch gates, but couldn't see yet.

Today she would track down Logan Winston and tell him he had a son. A precious seven-year-old who was Logan's self-proclaimed number one fan. And then she'd tell Cody who his father was.

She'd needed yesterday to sit with it. To plan *how* she'd tell Cody. But of course, there was only one way. She just had to tell him.

Tonight, after dinner, this child, this sweet, precious little boy she loved more than anything, would have his entire life shifted. Given who his father was, the news would be welcome, she assumed. But there would be questions.

Why didn't you tell me?

How could you not have told me?

Then she'd get in touch with Logan Winston.

Why didn't you tell me?

How could you not have told me?

Tears pricked the backs of her eyes. She didn't have good answers to that question.

This morning, she'd gotten at least ten emails and ten texts and three phone calls about Cody's photo and essay on the front page of the *Wyoming Gazette*, which had been accompanied by an article about Logan Winston and a wrist injury he'd gotten a couple days ago.

She could see the bus now, and her heart started pounding.

Cody, I have something to tell you.

Maybe she should tell him before dinner. The news would be so big that he wouldn't be able to eat, maybe. She could wait till after dinner, but then he might not be able to settle down to sleep.

Tomorrow was Saturday. She wouldn't have to worry about him getting to bed on time—his weekend bedtime was a half hour later. Or sending him off on the bus in the morning with such monumental news crowding his heart, mind and soul. They'd have the whole day together to talk about it and she'd be there to answer any questions.

And she'd get in touch with Logan.

Her heart hammered even harder.

Annabel sucked in a breath as the bus squealed to a stop, the big red stop sign swinging out, the door opening and Cody jumping out.

"Mommy! Guess what?" he exclaimed, just like yesterday.

And just like yesterday, she smiled at her son—though today she had to force it out of herself—waved at the bus driver, who then turned the bus back up the drive, and sucked in some of the very fresh spring air.

Cody ran to the bench again, dropped his backpack, pulled out the take-home folder and handed it to her.

A photocopy of the *Gazette* was right in front. A sticky note with *Wow!* from Ms. Gattano was above Cody's photo. He held up his essay with a big smile, his two front teeth adorably missing. Beside his photo was the short essay. And to the left of the photo was a long article about Logan Winston and the injury he'd sustained during a practice run two days ago.

There was a photo of Logan, too. On a bull, one hand on the rope, one in the air, the bull bucking. She was glad she couldn't see his face too well; he was in profile, for one, and his trademark black Stetson with the silver band around it shielded it.

But she remembered *him*. Oh, did she.

All day she'd wondered if he would see the newspaper. If he would connect the dots. If it would occur to him that Cody Dawson, age seven, could be Annabel Dawson's child.

And do the math.

She mentally shook her head. Doubtful. Not with all the Dawsons in Bear Ridge. He'd just assume he was one of her cousins' kids.

Then again, maybe any minute she'd be getting a call from a tall, dark-haired bull rider with intense blue eyes.

Unlike some people, Annabel Dawson was very easy to get a hold of.

But the paper had come out early this morning and now it was three forty-five. No call.

No matter. After she told Cody who his father was, she was going to track down Logan Winston herself and tell him he had a son he never knew about.

Last night, barely able to sleep, she'd grabbed her laptop in bed and gone to Logan's website, looking for contact information. There was an entire section devoted to how fans could contact him using a digital form.

She supposed she'd have to go that route, though it bugged her. She'd have preferred a direct email address, even if it was monitored by a member of his "team," the way she was sure his social media was. She couldn't even begin to imagine how many people filled out that form every day. Would it even get read? Would Logan actually see it? She was sure there were many forms from people who claimed that

"Logan and I used to know each other." Even if she wrote that she had something important to discuss with him, she doubted that would mean anything to the person in charge of sifting through the incoming forms. Would she have to chase Logan down? Figure out where he'd be later today or tomorrow and go charging over?

If she had to, she would.

Just as the bus disappeared from view, a very shiny red Range Rover came barreling down. A new set of guests, most likely.

"Ooh, Mommy, I like that car," Cody said, pointing.

The SUV stopped right in front of the open gates. That was weird. Why not drive through and stop at the Welcome Hut, where the attendant, Katie, would greet them at the side window.

A man got out of the passenger side. A very familiar man with tousled dark hair and intense blue eyes.

Annabel froze. She couldn't breathe. Couldn't move. Couldn't speak.

Logan Winston.

He was standing not ten feet away from her.

Staring at her. Now staring at Cody.

Now staring at her again.

Did he know? *Had* he connected the very unlikely, random, but absolutely on-target dots?

Why else would he be here?

He wore his trademark Stetson, black with the

studded silver band. And a fancy belt buckle with a bull etched in bronze.

"Logan Winston!" Cody screamed at the top of his lungs and burst into tears, alternating between jumping up and down and appearing completely shell-shocked.

Annabel could not find her voice.

It really was him.

He was here.

He *had* seen the front page of the *Gazette*.

He was here to claim his son?

His gaze shifted to Annabel for a moment, then went back to Cody. "It's me, all right," he said with a smile. "I'm here to see you, Cody." He looked at Cody—hard, she thought. "I recognize you from your picture in the newspaper today."

Annabel moved slightly forward, blocking Cody a bit with her body.

Logan raised an eyebrow at her. "Nice to see you again, Annabel."

Cody gasped and scrambled out from behind her. He stared from Logan to her. "Mommy, do *you* know Logan Winston?"

She swallowed against the lump in her throat. "I did know him—just briefly—back when he lived in Bear Ridge," she said fast.

Cody ran up to Logan. "You said you're here to see me? Because you saw my essay about you in the newspaper?"

Logan knelt down in front of Cody. "That's exactly why. I read your essay and thought it was great. So I came to meet you and answer your big question."

Cody's eyes widened. "About what you say to the bulls?"

"Yup. I say a lot to them."

Cody gasped again. "So awesome! I can't believe you're here! Mommy, Logan Winston is here!"

"He is," was all that would come out of Annabel's mouth. In a kind of squeak.

She still wasn't sure if he *knew*. If he *didn't* know, a little fan's essay had brought a big-time bull-rider here? To the town he hadn't returned to in eight years? Even when his father died?

He *wants* to know, she realized. That was why he was here. He thinks it's possible and wants to know for sure.

Well, you weren't looking forward to filling out that digital Contact Me form, and now you won't have to...

Logan's gaze landed on her again.

He looked the same. A bit more adult than the twenty-one-year-old he'd been. But that same gorgeous face, those deep blue eyes and sexy physique. He wore dark jeans, an olive-colored Henley and brown cowboy boots. He definitely had a rustic-glam quality—and he seemed both familiar and like a stranger. Like she must seem to him. She knew she looked just the same, if a little older herself.

He was staring at Cody—hard again. Looking for a resemblance to him? Cody didn't look much like Logan; he definitely took after Annabel with his light brown hair and fair complexion and fine features. And he had his grandfather Dawson's hazel eyes. But there was something in his features that was Logan Winston. Something in his expressions, the shape of his eyes, too.

A tall red-haired woman stuck her head out of the driver's side window of the Range Rover. "Um, Logan? I don't know why in tarnation you insisted we stop right here and flew out of the car, but can we pull in or what?"

Because he recognized me, Annabel knew. *And given that Cody's photo had been on the front page of the* Gazette *today, he realized I* was *Cody Dawson's mother. His self-proclaimed biggest fan whose photo and essay were right on the front page of today's Gazette.*

And that he could be Cody's father.

Of course, she had no idea if any of this was in Logan's head. She didn't know him at all. She might have once, a long time ago, even though their romance had been very short. But she didn't know *this* man.

Logan waved the car in. The redhead pulled up along the side and parked, then stepped out. She came over to her and Cody with a warm smile. She wore a white pantsuit and pale pink cowboy boots—

unusual choices for a visit to a ranch. She waved at the tinted windows of the back seat and a man came out of the back with a camera, a real camera, not just a cell phone.

"Well, hi there, li'l partner," the woman said to Cody, extending her hand, which Cody shook. "Now that I see you up close, I know just who you are! You're Cody Dawson—Logan Winston's number one little fan. I recognize you from your photo in today's *Wyoming Gazette*."

"That's right!" Cody said, beaming at the woman.

"I'm Savannah Walsh, Logan's manager," she continued. "After reading your essay, I had the best idea. Logan has a sprained wrist and has to rest up for a week before the big tournament in Cheyenne, and he's gonna do that right here. At the guest ranch where his number one little fan lives! That way, you two can get to know each other."

Cody's eyes widened. "Here? That's amazing! But I'm sorry your wrist got hurt."

Logan grinned. "I like the way you put that. Makes it sound like it wasn't my fault."

Savannah turned to Annabel. "Ma'am, are you Cody's mom?"

She slid a quick glance at Logan. He was staring at her. Waiting. For the confirmation.

Annabel took a quick deep breath. "Yes. Annabel Dawson. I work here at the ranch—leading wilderness tours in the woods and up Clover Mountain.

The Dawsons who own this place are cousins." She was rambling, which she always did when she was nervous.

She couldn't bring herself to look at Logan. To see the question in his eyes. But she could feel his gaze boring into her.

"It's a beautiful place," Savannah said, gazing around with a nod. "With your permission, we'd like to interview Cody about his wonderful essay and get a few photos of him and Logan. We'll share them on Logan's website and social media. Oh boy, will his fans love that! Logan spending some quality time with the young boy who wrote a school essay about him as his hero. So sweet!"

Wait a minute. Annabel was getting the feeling that while Logan might be wondering if Cody was his child, his manager had no clue. No clue of *any* connection between him and Cody—or her. Yes, Annabel was pretty sure that Savannah Walsh had suggested this entire thing as a photo op to counterbalance the slant of today's article that Logan Winston's injury might prevent him from defending his title as state bull-riding champion a little over a week from now. She'd heard a bunch of people talking about the article during her tours today.

Savannah had brought Logan here for the spin possibilities. Logan had agreed because of *other* possibilities. Suddenly, it all made sense.

"What do you think, Ms. Dawson?" Savannah

asked, her gaze boring into Annabel's. *You will say yes*, the shrewd brown eyes seemed to be saying.

Can we just hold on a minute? Can we just take a breath and a step back and let me actually process that this is all happening...

That Logan is here.

That he quite possibly knows already. Or suspects.

She took that deep breath. That was all she was going to get, she knew.

Annabel turned to her son. "How's that sound, Cody? Would you like that?" As if she needed to ask.

"Yes!" Cody said, jumping again.

The photographer directed Cody and Logan over to the gates, getting a shot of them in front of the Dawson Family Guest Ranch sign. If Logan was anxious, he wasn't showing it.

He was a professional, and this was a publicity thing.

Annabel swallowed again. Logan and Cody. Standing side by side. Logan sliding his arm around *their* son's narrow shoulder. Logan and Cody looking at each other and smiling.

"Ha, you thought this place was hard to book now?" Savannah said, "Wait till this photo goes out. Your cousins will be booking reservations for the next five years."

Annabel had no doubt. Logan Winston was that popular, that big a deal in western rodeo.

"I saw on the ranch's website that there's a petting zoo," Savannah said. "One of my sisters has a toddler—I'll bet they've been here," she added, looking a bit wistful for a moment. "Why don't we get some cute shots there. People will eat that up."

"They're going to eat the picture?" Cody asked, looking from Savannah to Logan.

"It's just a saying," Annabel explained. Logan smiled, then his expression tightened. He was definitely back to wondering.

A sadness came rushing up. *He is your child. And neither of you knows it yet.*

That was wrong. And she was going to fix it.

Once Logan was settled in his cabin, she'd knock on the door and tell him they needed to talk. Unless there were a bodyguard out front, keeping people back.

Sure, lady. Sure you have his secret child and need to tell him. Now run along with your delusions before I call the police.

Savannah and the photographer started getting back in the red SUV. "We can all fit in here," she said, waving them over.

"Actually, you can't park there," Annabel said, pointing to the sign marked Ranch Parking. "Only ranch vehicles are allowed on the paths—for safety."

"Oh," Savannah said. "I guess we're hoofing it!" she added with a laugh, sticking out her leg. Annabel coveted the pink cowboy boots she wore even though they definitely weren't dude ranch friendly. "How busy is the ranch about now?" she asked. "Just want to prepare, make sure our trusty photographer here has his camera ready to shoot some video of people running to see him."

"Most of the guests are on a horseback riding trip right now," Annabel said. "And the petting zoo won't get busy for about another half hour with the public after-school visitors, so it'll be quiet, actually."

Savannah frowned, then brightened. "Ah, no big whoop. We really just need our number one fan and he's right here." She grinned at Cody.

Though there was something definitely slick about Logan's manager, Annabel couldn't help but like her. She seemed like a straight shooter.

Logan slid on aviator sunglasses, and they headed up the path, past the old foreman's cabin and then the big white main house up atop the hill where Annabel's cousin Daisy, the guest relations manager, lived with her husband and children. Annabel had walked every inch of the Dawson Family Guest Ranch, and it never got old for her. The land that stretched as far as you could see, the ledges, the mountain in the distance, the enormous trees, the beautiful stables and barns. The various livestock grazing in the pastures, the big petting zoo, the cowboys on horseback dotted around. Annabel pointed out various spots to the surprise visitors, where the path to the guest cabins were along the river, where the cafeteria and lodge were. She loved leading her tours of the ranch and then heading past the trailhead into the woods and the mountain cliffs with various loops of different mileage and inclines and general difficulty.

The VIP cabins weren't far from her own cabin— the first was a quarter mile away, and they were a quarter mile apart from one another, tucked away into the woods so they couldn't be seen from any of the walking paths. Logan would be staying in one like the wealthy celebrity he was. Last week a well-known country singer had come with his family, one of his twin sons throwing a major tantrum on her tour through the woods. The boy did not like insects. Or walking. And last month, an actress whom Annabel had long admired had stayed a week on her own, taking long hikes in giant white pearl sunglasses and riding almost every horse in the stables. The Dawson Family Guest Ranch was a good place to recharge, and since there were only six guest cabins and the three VIP luxe cabins with concierge service that cost a fortune, there was privacy for those who sought it.

"So your cousins rebuilt this ranch?" Logan asked her. "I remember years ago the original Dawson Family Guest Ranch was abandoned and completely run-down. Bored teens, like myself, with nothing better to do used to sneak onto the property to hang out."

Annabel nodded. "The Dawsons who own the

place are siblings—there are six of them. They completely rebuilt the ranch their grandparents started. They're all married with kids now, so there are a lot of Dawsons on the property."

"I'm a Dawson," Cody said proudly, his attention then taken by a huge white butterfly that he zigzagged ahead after.

Logan moved to her side. "Guess you kept your maiden name, then?" he said in a low voice. "For Cody, too."

Ah, there it was. He was asking if she was married, if she'd met someone right after he left and Cody was *that* man's son. That nonexistent man. There'd been no one after Logan for a long, long time. And then just some short-lived romances. "I'm not married. It's just always been me and Cody," she whispered back. But she held his gaze for a moment. Telling him something.

He stared at her, his expression something close to shock, but then it quickly went neutral.

His gaze shot from her to Cody and back to her, his eyes widening again. "We'll talk after the shoot and interview?" he asked.

She nodded.

"What's all this whispering?" Savannah asked, eyeing them. "You two go way back?"

"We…briefly dated," Logan said, staring at Annabel.

"What?" Cody asked, stopping in the path and

running back to them. "You dated? You were boyfriend-girlfriend?"

"I wouldn't say *that*," Annabel said. "We just spent a little time together—a few days. Before you were born. Then Logan left town to become a bull rider and I never saw him again."

"Till now," Logan said, his gaze burning on her.

"Till now," she whispered.

A *baa* could be heard from just up ahead. Then another. The petting zoo animals always had a way of saving her from uncomfortable moments by turning the attention onto their cuteness.

Savannah rushed ahead at the sound. "Ah, perfect spot for the shoot!" she called, waving at them to hurry across the wide road to the petting zoo set up just outside a barn. "We'll get one right in front of the fence with those supercute goats on the log behind you two."

"The white one is my favorite," Cody said. "His name is Oinky."

"That sounds like the perfect name for a little piggy," the photographer said with a grin.

"The Dawson kids get to name the petting zoo animals," Cody added. "I named two chickens— Bucky for bucking bulls and Chappy for the chaps bull riders wear."

"Chappy the chicken," Logan said with a grin. "I like it."

Cody grinned. "Hey, I just thought of something.

You're the GOAT of bull riders. And the goats are *real* goats."

"They're the GOAT of goats," Logan said on a chuckle.

"But if they don't like you and you get too close, they'll eat your hair," Cody said.

Logan laughed. "I will definitely remember that."

And then Savannah was directing the shoot, the photographer butting heads with her a bit on angles. She had the guy take several of Logan and Cody next to each other, Cody standing up on a bench in front of the fence, his elbow on Logan's shoulder.

"Darn, I wish I could get one of Cody actually sitting on Logan's shoulders," Savannah said, "but I'm not risking Logan's wrist to finagle that for a good shot."

Annabel could swear Logan swallowed just then. And she doubted it was about his wrist and the idea of further injuring it while hoisting a little kid on his shoulder.

It was about the thought of hoisting *his son* on his shoulder.

He *knew.* Or was 99 percent sure and just had to ask the question.

Which was coming right after this.

"Okay, we've got our killer shot," Savannah said. "Now, Cody, I'd like to ask you a few questions. They'll run in quotes across the photos."

"So cool!" Cody said. "Ask me anything!"

"So now that you've met your hero, Logan Winston," Savannah began, "what do you think of him?"

Cody smiled up at Logan, then looked at Savannah. "I think I'm the luckiest kid in the whole world. It's not even my birthday and he's here! Logan Winston is just the best."

"You're gonna give me a big head," Logan said, and again, Annabel caught the slight swallowing.

"Your head isn't big," Cody said, tilting his own and eyeing Logan's.

Logan laughed again. "It's just another saying. For when you get a really good compliment."

"Ooh, Cody," Savannah said. "One last question. What do you want to be when you grow up?"

"I want to be a bull rider just like Logan Winston!" Cody said.

Savannah held up her hand for a high five, and Cody slapped her one. "Kids are the best," she said. "Well, we're outta here. Logan, I'll leave your luggage at the Welcome Hut. The concierge will deliver it to your cabin. And like Doc Russo said, do not, I repeat, do not lift anything heavier than a tissue with your right hand. Not even a curly fry. And certainly not the rein on a horse—it's the motion that'll do you in. Got it?"

"Got it," Logan said.

Savannah gave a shrewd nod. "I wish I could spend some time in town but I've got a slew of meetings. I'll check in, Logan." She turned to Cody and Annabel. "Great meeting you both. Take good care of my champ, okay?" she added to Cody.

"I will!" he said proudly.

With that, Savannah and the photographer headed back down the path toward the gates.

Logan was staring at her. Cody was staring at Logan, stars and hearts in his eyes.

Now it really *was* time.

Chapter Four

Logan wanted to ask Annabel straight-out right now if Cody was his child, but he couldn't when the boy was standing next to him, telling him the names of all the animals in the petting zoo.

The more he thought about it, the more he knew Cody had to be his. The timing said he was. He'd barely gotten through thinking *but why didn't she tell me* when he remembered how he'd disconnected his cell phone and disappeared, no way for anyone to get in touch. He didn't start placing in competitions for six months after that. Then he would have been easily findable—his events were posted on social media, on the website Savannah made him. But Annabel would have been heavily pregnant by then and maybe she'd just given up on the idea of him as her baby's father.

"Annabel, Cody!" a woman's voice called, and they all turned toward the petting zoo barn door, where a blonde woman in a Dawson's Family Ranch polo shirt like Annabel's and a toddler in each hand was exiting.

"Coey!" the tiny girl toddler said. She couldn't be older than a year and a half, not that Logan could really say.

"Cody!" the other one corrected. Logan would say the boy was three, tops.

He pushed his hat slightly down lower on his head, glad he had on his sunglasses. He wasn't up for introductions right now. Which Annabel seemed to recognize.

"So guess who has her hands completely full," the woman said, "but who nonetheless has a new puppy? Cody, want to come meet him? His name is Sparkles and he's supercute."

Cody's eyes lit up. But then he looked up at Logan and he had stars in his eyes. He bit his lip.

"Hey, Cody," Annabel said. "Why don't you go with Daisy and the kids and meet Sparkles the pup, and I'll pick you up in exactly an hour and you can hang out with Logan a bit more." She turned toward him. "If that's okay?"

Logan noticed Daisy was staring at him. He had a feeling she knew who he was but was giving him privacy. "Sounds great to me. I'll see you later for sure, Cody."

"Yay!" Cody said. Then he flung himself at Logan and wrapped his arms around the tops of Logan's legs.

Logan reached down to hug Cody back, his heart slightly pounding and doing all sorts of weird things in his chest.

The blonde woman eyed him, then looked at Annabel. "See you in an hour," she said with a smile and a firm nod as if she seemed to understand there was some unfinished business between him and Annabel.

They both stood there, in front of the goats, as the group of four walked toward the house on the hill, the boys running in zigzags, Daisy and her younger toddler taking it slower. Then Logan turned to Annabel.

"Is Cody my child?" he asked, almost holding his breath.

She would say no, right? She'd say that she'd started seeing someone else right after he fled town. That she'd gotten pregnant, and the relationship hadn't worked out. Because there was no way that Logan Winston was meant to be anyone's father.

He'd meant what he'd said back then, about never wanting children. He'd always known he wouldn't have a family of his own. There were people to whom family was everything. And then there was Logan, who knew that family meant trouble, heartache and loss. The ones you couldn't bear to lose—they left you. The ones you wished would go far, far away? They stuck around for a long time. Like his father. Until they, too, were gone and you couldn't understand why you were out of sorts about it.

She sucked in a breath. "My cabin is right there," she said, pointing across the road. "Let's talk there."

He almost breathed a sigh of relief that she didn't answer. What if the answer was yes?

What then?

They walked across the road to the two-story cabin that was tucked away in the tree line. He was consumed by the need to know, his feet itching to stop and ask again, but he told himself to let it go for the two minutes it would take to reach a place where they could talk privately.

Once inside, his attention was taken by the artwork that greeted him in the entryway, captioned Self Portrait, Cody Dawson, Age 5. Cody had given himself a square head and oddly placed ears but otherwise, the pastel drawing kind of looked like him.

Are you my son? he silently asked the portrait.

"Let's talk in the kitchen," she said. "I need coffee. I have great pineapple sparkling water, too."

"The pineapple drink sounds good," he said, following her into the small room. He sat down at the round table by the window, watching her as she went to the refrigerator and took out the can of pineapple water and set it on the table with a glass. She did not look at him once.

Because Cody was his.

A strange fear came over him, a shiver going up his spine.

Now Annabel was by the coffee maker, pouring grinds in the filter basket. She kept her back to him as she hit the brew button.

"You can answer my question while you wait for the coffee to brew," he said. Maybe too harshly. But she still hadn't answered, and his chest was about to explode.

She turned to face him, her hands braced on the counter behind her. "Yes, he's your son."

The air whooshed out of his lungs. If he tried to stand, his knees would buckle—that was how suddenly weak he felt.

"The day I found out I was pregnant, I broke down and told my mom—not your name or any details, just that I'd dated the baby's father only a few days before he'd suddenly left town. She told me to call you and tell you, no matter what. So I tried. But your number was disconnected."

He closed his eyes for a moment. "I wanted to cut all ties to Bear Ridge. The bad and the good. You were the good, Annabel."

She turned toward the coffee maker. "I tried googling you a few times as the weeks wore on, but your name never came up. Then I just accepted what was, you know? That you were gone and didn't want to be found. And in my head, I would constantly hear you saying that you never wanted kids. *Ever.*"

He had said that. Continue his father's line? Back then, that was a hard no. Apparently, Logan's paternal grandfather hadn't been an easy person to get along with, either. Cody seemed like pure sunshine, but maybe all young kids were. The ones who ran up to Logan all the time sure were. He tried to imagine his father at seven, all smiley and full of excitement, but Logan couldn't see it. Everett Winston had probably been a little bully just as he'd been a big bully.

Logan cracked open the can of pineapple fizzy water and took a long drink. His throat was still parched, his nerve endings frayed.

Annabel turned to face him, wringing her hands, stuffing them in her pockets, pulling them out again. "Then when I saw you on the cover of the free weekly and that you'd won a bunch of competitions, I didn't know what to do. It had been more than six months since you'd left. Your dreams were coming true. I was going to call you and tell you I had something of yours that you said you never wanted back in the town you hated?"

Shame rushed into his gut and he almost choked on the pineapple water. "I—" He had no idea what to say to that. He understood.

No one had ever cared about his dreams. Or how

his life was going. Well, except Savannah, even seven years ago when she'd only spotted his *potential*.

"You said outright that you never wanted kids," she added. "And then there you were, winning competition after competition, becoming a champ. Beautiful women in lots of photos of you on social media. I felt a million miles away from you in every regard."

And she'd been only eighteen. He was grateful that her parents had been so supportive. "I'm sorry I put you in that position, Annabel. Very sorry. I understand why you didn't tell me."

The coffee maker pinged, and she turned back toward it but didn't reach for a mug. "It was wrong, though," she finally said, turning around again. "Wrong to do to Cody. Wrong to do to you, even if it wasn't what you wanted, even if it would have stuck a monkey wrench in your plans. You had the right to know. But I didn't give you the choice."

"Because you cared about me," he said slowly.

"Because I cared about you," she confirmed. "And the more time went by, the bigger you became, the more lost to me you seemed. The more it seemed like the Logan I knew for three days and the Logan Winston who was Wyoming's superstar and every kid's hero weren't the same."

"Oh, Annabel," he said, feeling like absolute hell. "I get it."

Her shoulders, which had seemed all bunched up a second ago, seemed to relax a bit at that. "The front page of the *Gazette* let me know it was time to tell Cody and you—long overdue, but time. I finally told my mom, and my plan was to tell Cody before dinner. And as for you, I figured I'd have to fill out that stupid form on your website and hope it reached you or I'd just drive to your next competition and storm the bull chute."

He gave her something of a smile, but then it faded. "Can I be there when you tell him?"

"Yes, of course. I can't even begin to imagine how he'll react. Happiness and shock in equal parts. But he'll want to know why I never told him till now. And that's going to be hard to explain to a seven-year-old."

"What have you said so far?" he asked, swigging the rest of his drink.

"Just that I only knew his father a very short time and he left town before I could tell him I was pregnant and I didn't know how to reach him."

Logan nodded.

"But then I *did* know," she said. "And I still didn't get in touch with you. How do I explain that in a way he understands? I've been his sole parent. He trusts me with every little thing. What's this going to do to *that*?" Her face crumpled and she covered it with her hands.

He bolted out of the chair and pulled her into his arms.

She seemed so surprised that she stopped crying

and just fell against him, her hands pressed against his chest.

For a moment, they stood like that, just hanging on to each other. She felt so good in his arms. Like she belonged there. Like a return of something that had been missing.

But then she stepped sideways, and so did he. She looked *very* uncomfortable.

"I'm okay," she said. "I mean, I'm not. But he has to know and I'll have to deal with the fallout."

"He's seven and loves you," Logan said. "Whatever you do say about why you didn't tell him, why you didn't find me when you could, he'll know you had your reasons and that'll be good enough for him, Annabel. If he were fourteen, it would be another story. But he's seven. And you're his world."

She bit her lip and then nodded, seeming slightly comforted by that. She reached into the cabinet for a mug and poured herself coffee, adding a sugar cube and some cream. She brought it over to the table and sat down, and he sat back down, too.

"I'll pick him up in a half hour—that was my cousin Daisy at the petting zoo, by the way. She's the guest relations manager here at the ranch and I have no doubt she knew exactly who you were and read between the lines so didn't bother with introductions. I'll bring Cody here or we can come to your cabin."

"I think we should tell him on his turf," Logan

said. "In his room. Where he's surrounded by all his stuff and feels comfortable."

She nodded. "For a man who never wanted kids and travels the rodeo for a living, you're sure good at this. Saying the right thing. Having the right answer."

He didn't know how he was pulling that off.

"It's a little easier from the outside," he said. "But I guess I'm not on the outside. I'm his father." He leaned his head back. "I'm someone's father."

Her gaze shot to his. "How does it feel?"

"Impossible," he said. "Me? A father." He let out a harsh breath. "But I am, nonetheless. Past aside. Things I said aside. I'm Cody's father and I plan to honor that in every way it should be."

She tilted her head and stared at him, her face slightly paling. "Meaning?"

"Meaning I'm his father and want to be in his life. We can work on how."

She slowly nodded, then shot up. "I'll go pick him up now, actually, instead of waiting. I'll text Daisy that you're ready to head over to your cabin. She'll send the VIP guest concierge over here right away and he'll golf-cart you to the cabin and give you the lay of the land. Expect not to do a single thing for yourself for the next week, other than breathe."

"Oh, I think I'll be doing a lot more than that," he said.

She bit her lip again, then hurried toward the door. "You can wait here for the concierge. Why don't you come back over at around six thirty? We'll tell him then."

He nodded slowly and then she was gone.

And then his knees really did buckle.

Meaning I'm his father and want to be in his life. We can work on how...

Annabel glanced at her phone on the kitchen counter: 6:22 p.m. Logan would be here in eight minutes. Cody would hear his voice at the door and go running up to him, all excited about spending more time with his hero. And then with one sentence, *Cody, Logan is your father*, their lives would completely change. All three of their lives.

Cody would have a lot of questions for them both. *She* had a lot of questions, starting with: Well, how *do* you see yourself fitting into Cody's life? Logan would be at the ranch for a week, which would make for an easy enough start. But what about when he left for Cheyenne? He'd go back to the road, back to competitions and training. He certainly wouldn't be in Cody's life on a daily basis. Competitions were often on weekends, and that was Cody's free time, though summer break would be here next month.

Then again, there had been *nothing* for seven years. Nothing where a father should be.

Anything would be an improvement.

Annabel had figured that she and Logan should let Cody know the big news after dinner, since he'd have a good two and a half hours of downtime before bed. Tomorrow was Saturday, which meant he wouldn't have to deal with school or getting up early. She never worked weekends, so she would be available to him all day for questions. And she was sure she'd have them. On the way to Daisy's to pick up Cody, she'd called her Mom and whispered all that happened and what was about to happen tonight.

If you need me, I'm here, her mom had said.

She eyed her phone. Six twenty-five. During dinner, which had been a homemade pizza with Cody's favorite toppings—meatball and red peppers—their Friday night tradition, Cody alternated between talk of Sparkles, Daisy's new puppy, a corgi mix who was truly adorable, and Logan. *He's so nice! He's so tall!* She'd told Cody he'd back after dinner, and Cody had run to his room to make a list of questions so that he wouldn't forget to ask anything he wanted to know. *What is your favorite color? What is your favorite food? Do you like vegetables? Are you ever scared? Did you have a lot of friends when you were a kid?*

The doorbell rang.

Annabel swallowed.

Cody went racing to the door. "Who's there, please?" he called out, as she'd taught him to do before ever unlocking the door without her beside him.

"It's Logan Winston."

Cody jumped and shot his fist in the air. He unlocked the door and opened it, and Annabel, standing a few feet behind Cody, almost gasped at the sight of him. He wore a tuxedo and shiny black leather shoes, a black bow tie, his thick dark hair brushed back like a movie star's. Or a champion bull rider's.

"Are you going to an event later or something?" she asked.

"Yeah," Cody said. "You must be getting a big award. For being the GOAT of bull riders!"

"Actually, I'm all dressed up to see you, Cody," Logan explained.

Now Annabel did gasp. He'd put on a tux to tell Cody that he was his father. *Because he knows that when Cody thinks back to this moment, he'll always remember that his father thought this was a very special occasion.* And it was.

She realized she was staring at Logan, and darted her gaze to Cody, who was still standing in the doorway. "Cody, how about you show Logan your room?"

"Okay! C'mon," Cody said, charging up the stairs.

"I'm ready if you're ready," she whispered to Logan.

"Ready as I'll ever be," he whispered back.

Yeah, same here, she thought, her heart starting to pound as she led the way to the stairs.

They followed Cody up to his room, the hallway barely wide enough for the two of them.

Annabel saw Logan's gaze go to the poster of himself on the wall just above Cody's bed. Cody pointed out all his things, from his tattered stuffed bull that he'd had since he was a baby to his scooter and the front page of the *Gazette* and his four old rodeo ticket stubs on his bulletin board.

"My granddaddy took me," Cody said, "But he died and so now my cousins Ford and Rex take me. They're policemen and superfans, too."

How she'd appreciated the first time Ford and Rex, who were indeed officers with the BRPD, and two of the six siblings who owned the ranch, offered to take Cody with them to Logan's first event after she'd lost her grandfather. The Dawson family was so thoughtful, so kind. She wasn't even from a close branch, but they'd always treated her as if she were. It had become a tradition for the trio to attend Logan's local events, so Cody had never pressed her to go; she liked that it was a "boys' day out" as it had been with his grandfather. She would have gone, if she had to. But it would have been rough.

"I'm sorry to hear about your granddaddy," Logan said.

Annabel felt Logan looking at her. "Cody, honey, why don't we sit down? We both want to talk to you about something important."

"Am I in trouble for something?" Cody asked.

"Nope. Nothing like that," Annabel assured him.

Cody sat on his bed and looked from her to Logan. Annabel sat beside him, and Logan took the chair at the desk and turned it toward them.

"Cody, the last few years you've been asking me lots of questions about your father and who he is and why he's not in your life," Annabel began. "I've always said that your father left town and I didn't know how to reach him to tell him about you."

"I know that, Mommy," Cody said, kind of frowning.

"Well, do you remember when you asked me what your father's name was?" Annabel went on, swallowing against the lump in her throat. "And I told you his name was Logan John?" She slid a glance to Logan, whose eyes slightly widened. "And you said you liked the idea that your father's name was the same first name as your hero?"

Cody nodded.

"Well, I didn't tell you your father's entire name. His first name is Logan and his middle name is John. His last name is Winston."

Cody tilted his head. "Like Logan Winston?" He looked at Logan. "My father has the same name as you!"

She glanced at Logan, who looked like his chest was going to explode. "Cody, honey, Logan Winston, sitting right there, is your father. I didn't tell you because he never knew, either. But now that he came home to Bear Ridge to meet you because of your essay, I knew it was time for you both to know." That was all true but sounded so…lacking.

She tried to blink back the tears forming.

Cody popped up and was now leaning against his

bed and staring at Logan, confusion on his little face. "You're my father? My real father?"

"Yes," Logan said with a firm nod. "I just found out today. Same as you."

Cody seemed very confused and bit his lip. He looked shyly at Logan, then at Annabel. He dropped down on the bed and grabbed his stuffed bull, holding it tight on his lap. "But why didn't you tell me, Mommy? You knew Logan Winston was my hero. Why didn't you tell me?"

A rush of sadness and shame lodged in Annabel's heart, and now the tears did come. "Cody, I—" she began, but what could she say that would make sense to her seven-year-old? She hadn't told him.

"I think I know why, Cody," Logan said, bringing his chair over to sit right across from Cody. "Almost eight years ago, when I met your mom, we dated for just three days. I really cared about your mom, but I was having a hard time here in Bear Ridge. I didn't get along with my dad and I was angry about a lot of stuff. So I just left town and I never came back. I changed my cell phone number. Your mom couldn't get in touch with me."

"Oh," Cody said, still frowning.

"And when I started making a name for myself as a bull rider," Logan went on, "your mom would have been able to find me to tell me about you. But she knew I didn't want a family. I know that's not nice to say, especially to you. But back then, it was true. I didn't have a good family life with my dad. So I didn't want a family of my own."

Cody bit his lip again. "What about now?"

"Now I'm a different person than I was then," Logan said. "Now I'm happy to know that I have a son. I'm sorry that I missed out on the first seven years of your life, Cody. Because you're a really great kid."

Cody burst into tears. He stood up, holding his stuffed bull, and then dropped down on his bed again, and for a second, Annabel was frozen. She was about to go over to him, put an arm around him, do *something*, when he flew at her, flinging his arms around her. She was so surprised that she almost burst into tears, too. He cried and wiped at his eyes, then looked up at her. "Is Logan Winston really my daddy?"

She blinked tears back. "Yes, he is."

He looked at Logan. "And you want to be my father now?"

She saw Logan swallow. He took a breath and then scooted his chair closer to Cody.

"Yes," Logan said. "You have my promise, Cody. I'm your father and I want to be."

Cody flung his bull on his bed and then ran to Logan and burrowed his face into his chest.

Logan hesitated for just a moment, then wrapped his arms around the boy and hugged him tight.

Annabel blinked back tears. How was her heart still inside her chest?

Cody sat back down on his bed. "Can I ask you some questions?"

Logan looked nervously at Annabel. "Sure. Anything."

Cody ran over to his desk and took the sheet of loose-leaf paper that had been facedown. He sat on his bed again and scanned the paper. "What is your favorite color?"

Logan laughed—and looked very relieved. "That's super easy. It's silver. Like the band around my cowboy hat. The day I met your mother, she was wearing a puffy silver coat. Silver's been my favorite color ever since."

Annabel was astonished. She had no idea. She never would have thought his trademark hat had anything to do with her.

Cody grinned. "I like silver, too." He glanced at the paper. "What is your favorite food?"

"Always and forever," Logan said. "A cheeseburger. Medium. With a really good bun, not too soft, and lettuce, tomato and lots of ketchup."

"I like ketchup on my cheeseburgers, too!" Cody exclaimed. "But not lettuce. Or tomatoes. And now I don't have to ask my next question cuz I already know. You *do* like vegetables."

Logan laughed. "And I like my cheeseburger with fries. Any kind. Skinny ones, steak fries, tater tots—I love my fries."

"Me, too!" Cody said, his eyes so bright and happy

that Annabel could cry. "I have three more ques-tions written down but I might think of more later, is that okay?"

"Yup. You can ask me as many questions as you want. Any time. And I have lots of questions for you, too. I want to know everything about you."

Cody beamed. "My next question is—did you have friends when you were a kid? I don't really have any except for my cousins. But they're all ei-ther lots younger than me or lots older."

"My only friends when I was a kid were the an-imals at the ranches I helped out on for spending money," Logan said.

Cody gasped. "Same as me! My friends are the goats and chickens. I talk to Bucky and Chappy a lot."

"Well, you know *I* talk to animals. Especially bulls. Even when they're mad they're still good friends."

Cody's eyes widened. "Yeah. I bet they are!"

Annabel did recall Logan mentioning a friend. A guy named CJ. She wondered if Logan had left him behind, too. Probably had.

"Ready for my next question?" Cody asked.

Annabel had a feeling that Logan probably needed to take a minute, gulp down some coffee or some fresh air. This had to be hard for him.

"Ready."

"Do you ever get scared? Or are bull riders not afraid of anything?"

"I sure do get scared. Everyone does."

"Wow, even Logan Winston," Cody said, eyes wide.

"Even me."

"So what do you do when you get scared?" Cody asked.

"Well, I try to stop and think about *why* I'm scared," Logan said. "Sometimes it's a sign that I shouldn't be doing something. And sometimes it's a sign that I *should*. It's hard to know the difference. But it gets me thinking about it."

Good answer, Annabel thought. That was exactly how she'd felt all day. And now.

Cody tilted his head. "I think I know what you mean. Like when I wanted to dive off the dock last summer but I was scared so I didn't. My mom said I'd be ready when I was ready. Maybe I'll be ready this summer."

"Your mom is exactly right," Logan said, sliding his gaze over to her.

"We're up to my last question," Cody said. "What I've wanted to know for the past two years! What *do* you say to the bulls when you're holding on for the eight seconds?"

Logan smiled. "I thank them for letting me have these eight seconds with them. And then I tell them that even though they're not going to throw me, they're awesome."

Cody beamed. "That's really nice of you to tell them."

It was.

Cody seemed happy, his heart and mind settled right now with the big news.

Annabel felt herself relax. She also felt Logan reach over and quickly squeeze her hand, then let go.

Suddenly she flashed back to their three days and was reminded of how he'd held her hand in bed. How they'd kissed for minutes at a time. How they'd seemed to have a connection and chemistry for no reason either could think of. They'd had nothing in common. But there'd been something so special between them. Her mind flashed to their embrace earlier. How comfortable she'd felt in his arms for those few seconds. How *un*comfortable she'd gotten because of that.

They weren't going to pick up where they left off. But while he'd held her, she'd definitely wondered.

Dangerous, Annabel. He left you once and he'll certainly leave you again. With anything brewing between you two or not.

As if there was anything brewing between them! Logan was a famous bull rider. She was the very sudden mother of his child. That's what she was to him. He probably had a serious girlfriend where he lived. Or a beautiful woman waiting in every port— rodeo town.

What she should remember was how hurt she'd been when she'd gotten his I'm-leaving-town-*bye* text. How alone she'd felt when she'd seen that orange plus sign in the little home pregnancy test window. How heartsick she'd been when she'd tried his cell phone with her mother standing at her side and discovered he'd changed the number.

How off-balance she'd been all this time because of her secret, because of the huge truth she was keeping from Logan and from her child.

Yup, this line of thinking helped. She wasn't flashing back to Clover Mountain with Logan. Or making love and running out of an entire box of condoms.

"Oh, guess what?" Cody said, popping up again and racing for his backpack on the side of his desk. He pulled out his take-home folder and opened it up, then handed a piece of paper to Logan. "You can help me fill this out!"

Logan scanned the paper, his expression shifting to what Annabel would describe as…discomfort.

"What's that?" Annabel asked, coming around to the other side of Logan to take a look. Ah. Now she knew what made Cody actually excited about an assignment on a Friday.

The sheet of paper was titled My Family Tree with instructions for students to draw a tree and use the branches to add family members. Parents. Grandparents. Great-grandparents. Aunts and uncles. Cousins. Chosen family.

"I asked Ms. Gattano what chosen family was," Cody said, pointing to the words, "and she said it's anyone who isn't a relative but feels like one. I'm putting down Oinky the goat, and Bucky and Chappy for that line."

Annabel had barely processed how lovely it was that the project included "chosen family," when she noticed Logan eyeing the homework assignment as though it were a rabid bat. About to bite. "Well, I think I know the basics for my side."

Cody was all smiles. "This mean kid told me I'd only be able to fill out half the tree cuz I don't have a dad. But now I do. And it's you!"

Logan smiled, too, but Annabel could plainly tell he was as affected as she was.

"I see kids haven't changed since I was in second grade," Logan said.

"Can we go to the store to buy the construction paper tomorrow?" Cody asked, looking from Annabel to Logan. "And then I can draw the tree and we can fill in the branches. Can we?"

"If it's okay with your mom," Logan said.

Annabel smiled at her son. *Their* son. "It's okay with me."

From telling Cody that Logan was his dad to jumping right in, full body.

"Oh," Cody said, biting his lip and looking shyly at Logan. "I just remembered that I do have one more question."

Logan tilted his head. "Ask me anything."

"Should I call you Daddy or Logan?"

Annabel could only describe Logan's immediate reaction as pure deer in headlights.

Chapter Five

Of all Cody's questions, Logan thought two hours later as he waited for Annabel in his cabin, that very last one was the toughest.

Should I call you Daddy or Logan?

A response hadn't easily come. Heart hammering, Logan had looked at Annabel, who seemed as unable to immediately answer as he was. But then he'd asked, *What feels right to you, Cody?*

Cody had chewed on his lip again. *I think I want to call you Logan for now.*

Logan had been relieved. Being called Daddy would feel very, very strange. Appropriate, but strange.

He'd given Cody a hug and said he'd see him tomorrow, then he'd left their cabin, his legs like Jell-O, his heart racing.

Nothing—no argument with his father, no bucking bull, no experience in his life—had shaken him quite like this.

The plan he and Annabel had made was that she'd put Cody to bed, answer any *more* questions he might have, and then once he was asleep, her mom would come over to babysit, and Annabel would walk over to his cabin, which was about a quarter mile away, so they could talk.

Namely about how this was going to work. Joint parenthood.

Sudden parenthood.

Logan couldn't even imagine. His life certainly wasn't set up for *any* kind of relationship, let alone a parent-child one. Not that he had any idea what was involved in that. Based on what he saw at the rodeo, particularly while families waited for autographs, parenting was...*intense*. Corralling impatient, super-excited young humans. On long lines were tears, requests, questions, sibling squabbles, fistfights and the occasional wander-away-er. Logan always signed the last autograph grateful as hell that he didn't have a kid. And sure he'd been right all those years ago when he'd told Annabel Dawson in the Starlight B and B that he'd didn't want kids—ever.

Right now, all he knew for absolute certain was that he did have a kid—and that he didn't want to get this wrong, any of it. Cody, sweet, honest, open, already had some kind of hold on him. Or was it just the word *father* that had its hooks into Logan?

Now, Logan was pacing in front of the living room windows, trees not quite fully bloomed still providing privacy, when Annabel's knock sounded. He opened the door to find her standing back a bit, expression strained, her hands shoved into the pockets on her white fleece pullover.

She'd changed her clothes. Along with the fleece she wore gray yoga pants and pale pink slip-on sneakers, her long blond hair pulled back in a ponytail. She looked so fresh-scrubbed and young, like the girl he'd remembered.

"You okay?" he asked, stepping onto the porch.

She shook her head, her light brown eyes full of so many emotions. But she didn't say anything. Or move.

"That was *a lot*," he offered. "Start to finish."

He'd had to decompress for a good hour when he'd gotten to the cabin. He'd grabbed a beer from the fridge and sat outside on the deck on a cushy chaise, grateful for the privacy since there was nothing to see but trees, nothing to hear but the sounds of the river a bit of a distance away. He'd just stared up at the night sky, barely able to believe what had happened today—from the news itself to the conversation with Cody. Logan felt a little more himself now; he'd done his usual thing of telling himself he'd just "take it day by day" and not overthink. But the only reason he wasn't overthinking was because he was *over*whelmed.

And now there was another conversation to have.

Annabel nodded, then dropped her head back and looked up at the sky, the stars dotting, the moon almost a crescent. She backed up a bit to lean against the railing. "Everything is different. Our lives from this point on—different. Mine, yours, Cody's. It's…" She leaned her head back again.

"Overwhelming," he said. Word of the day. Of the moment.

She nodded again. "It's been just me and Cody for a long time. Now it's not just us. And I don't know what things will be like from here on in. I don't know how our lives will change."

I don't know either. "Well, know this—the most important thing to me is to be in Cody's life. I'm not sure what that means on a daily basis either. I don't know anything about being a dad, Annabel."

"You're good at talking to him, though," she said. "The way you answered his questions—about why I never told him about you—that was just right."

Huh. "That means a lot to me. That I'm not messing this up from the get-go."

"You're definitely not. In fact, you're being…great. About everything."

"That might be a first," he said without meaning to. Then felt like he had to continue the thought. "I'm usually told I'm distant. Uncommunicative. Noncommittal."

She tilted her head. "So no girlfriend waiting at home. Or hidden upstairs in the master bedroom." She gave him something of a smile and made a show of peering past him into the cabin.

That got a smile out of him, too. "Hardly. 'Girlfriend' and my life don't go together. I'm on the road *a lot*."

She eyed him for a second, then pushed off from the railing. "I guess it'll be the same where Cody's concerned?"

He let out a breath. "I really don't know. We definitely need to talk this all through." He held the door open wide. "Come on in. I have a refrigerator full of food and beverages, thanks to either my manager or the concierge. Someone went shopping for me and stocked it with my favorites."

She stepped inside. "I remember you always wanting pizza with sausage and peppers."

He found himself smiling again and closed the door behind her. "That hasn't changed. One of the few things I've missed about Bear Ridge is Toni and Tony's Pizzeria. Still the best I've ever had." He'd spent a lot of time there as a teenager. The married couple who owned the place were among the few who'd treated him with respect back then instead of expecting him to rob the place at any minute.

His father had loved Toni and Tony's, too. Maybe the only thing they ever had in common.

"It's still there," Annabel said, her hands back in the fleece's front pockets. "Same hole-in-the-wall place. Same line out the door. I asked Toni if she and Tony were thinking about moving into a bigger location, and she said, 'Why mess with perfection?' Apparently they put all their money into the best ingredients and hiring good employees."

"Maybe the three of us could go there tomorrow," he said. "You, me and Cody."

She nodded, shyly, he thought, then looked around as she stepped farther into the cabin. "I've been in the VIP cabins, but whoa—they're definitely luxe."

Logan liked luxe. Another word that didn't conjure up home or his father. Polished hardwood floors. Interesting area rugs. Plush leather-and-suede sofas and love seats. A huge stone fireplace. Pale gray walls with abstract paintings and illustrations of all things dude ranch—horses, the mountain range, cowboys. State-of-the-art kitchen, swank bathroom with quite possibly the softest towels he'd ever had against his face. And since he'd splashed cold water on that face when he'd gotten back from Annabel's, he'd appreciated the plush apricot-hued towels. He had no doubt the bedroom would have blackout shades, very high thread-count sheets, and very soft down pillows. He was looking forward to that—bed.

Where he could close his eyes and finally let himself process everything that had happened today.

"And now it's my turn to offer you fruit water," he said. "My fridge and freezer are stocked if you're hungry. Savannah makes things happen. Might even be a pizza from T&T's in there," he added.

Her expression changed for a moment as if she seemed to be remembering something. They'd eaten at the pizza joint twice in the three days they'd spent together.

"I don't think I could eat a bite," she said, sitting down on one of the cushy armchairs across from the brown leather sofa. She hugged a throw pillow to her stomach, just like Cody had with his stuffed bull not too long ago. "Just a drink, please. Fruit water of some kind sounds good."

He went into the kitchen and came back with two small, squat bottles of coconut-lime sparkling water. "Hmm, not sure how *this* concoction got on any grocery list of mine," he said, eyeing the label suspiciously as he handed her one. "Sometimes Savannah pushes her favorites on me."

Annabel smiled and they sipped, made a little small talk about the up-and-down early June weather, when it could be cold or warm, and then Logan said, "So I was thinking the three of us could go school supply shopping tomorrow morning, then work on the project."

She nodded. "Cody will be excited for that." She

took a long sip of her drink. "Not bad," she said, holding up the bottle. "I'd buy this. I remember you had a thing for lemonade, though. Homemade."

He nodded. "Still do. My mom used to always have a pitcher of fresh-made lemonade in the fridge. Lemons, sugar, water, ice. Especially after she died, a glass of cold lemonade would make me really sad and really comforted at the same time."

"I know what you mean. Same with me and my grandfather's Sunday night green chile chicken burritos, a family tradition since I was little. My mom keeps it up and her burritos taste just the same. Sometimes I miss him so much at Sunday dinner I cry happy tears over those burritos."

He wanted to walk over to her and scoop her into his arms and just hold her. Tell her he *knew*. There were times at his condo or on the road when he'd need to get his head straight, and he'd go find a river to sit in front of and let himself remember his mother, a stabilizing force in his life. Let himself miss her. Ask himself what she'd say in response to this or that.

He had no doubt what she'd say about *this*—about his sudden son. *Be the father you wish you had.*

He just wasn't quite sure how to do that without having seen it firsthand. He knew what *not* to do. But not exactly what *to* do.

"For a long time when I left Bear Ridge I avoided anything that reminded me of home," he said. "Luckily no sausage and pepper pizza was as good as

T&T's, so I could eat that all I wanted and not get all riled up."

He frowned, wondering why he was talking so much about himself. About the past. They were supposed to focus on the here and now. After his mother died when he was ten, his father rarely cooked except for a weekly huge pot of overdone spaghetti and jarred sauce, and to this day, Logan couldn't stomach spaghetti in marinara. Years ago, back when he had no idea how to conduct himself on an interview, how to actually answer questions the *right* way—meaning social media friendly—while still being honest, Savannah had had to coach him on talking about Bear Ridge and his likes and dislikes to the press. Once, before she knew even the little she did about his past, she'd said, *Logan John Winston, you're the least nostalgic person I've ever met.*

He frowned, realizing one of his worries about coming back to Bear Ridge, staying here, had reared its ugly head. He was thinking about the past.

So just get your mind back on Cody.

He took out his phone and opened up the notes app to jot down what he'd need to know and remember, setting it on his knee. "Okay, so what do I need to know about Cody?"

She set down her drink, sat back and clasped her hands on her lap. "What do you mean?"

"What is involved? In being a parent on a daily

basis, I mean. I'm assuming there's some kind of schedule."

She tilted her head. "Well, the schedule isn't what it used to be when Cody was a toddler and not in school seven hours a day. But yes, there's a schedule. Some days it's worthless. Some days I depend on it not to fall apart. Some days it actually goes smoothly."

He raised an eyebrow. "Well, would what constitute a monkey wrench?"

"A bad dream causing him to be late for the bus, so I'd need to drive him to school, which is a good half hour away, and there goes an unexpected hour from my workday. Which means calling in and letting people know. Making up the time. Or there's a stomachache at school and me needing to drop everything to go pick up Cody. Or asking my mom to. And because I know she will drop everything for me and Cody, I try not to ask her too much. She already gives way too much and I don't want to take advantage, you know?"

"I honestly *don't* know," he said. "Savannah snaps her fingers and things happen for me—because of money. And my name," he added. Now *that* had been easy to get used to. Logan wouldn't say he took the perks of his life for granted, but he sure did enjoy them.

"There's definitely no finger snapping and things magically appearing around here." She smiled.

"Sometimes I fantasize about that. When a wilderness tour goes awry or an unexpected wild animal staring at us takes everything out of me and then I get home, hungry and tired, to a hungry kid, I wish I could make a decent dinner appear like magic on my table."

Couldn't be easy being a single parent. His mother had been married to his father till the day Logan lost her, but she could never make ends meet and died with a lot of credit card debt. His father didn't even try. Dinner would be heated up from the weekly pot of spaghetti or whatever Logan could scrounge up, but it was usually a slice of $1.99 pizza from coins he'd find around the house or from his paycheck as a newspaper delivery boy and later a busboy. When he became a ranch hand, he started to eat a lot better since there was a cafeteria at the big ranches he worked at and the job came with room and board.

If Logan could snap his fingers for himself, he'd damned well do the same for Annabel and Cody.

"Well, anything you need, you just tell me. And I'm here to help," Logan said. "Any of those monkey wrenches come up, I'm here."

"For the next week, anyway." There was an edge to her voice suddenly.

"Right," he said. "But I'll certainly make things financially easier. About hiring sitters or whatever you need."

She stared at him. "Yeah, that's what I thought."

"Meaning?" he asked, putting his bottle down on the coffee table.

"Why don't we talk logistics," she said, her light brown eyes hard on him. "You'll be here for a week, cement a relationship with Cody, then hit the road. What is your plan for visitation?"

"I hadn't thought about it yet, but let's talk that out now. I want to do right by him, Annabel."

Her expression softened. "Sorry. You just found out about Cody. And you handled that news and him really beautifully, Logan. I don't mean to rush you about logistics. But I guess I'm a little uneasy about… everything. All the changes this is going to mean. In good ways and hard ways."

"What would be a hard way?" he asked. "I want to know so that I can ease the path from the get-go."

"Let's say Cody wants something and I say no, sorry, for this or that reason. But now I'm not the sole parent. Sole decision maker. It'll occur to him he can just go ask Daddy and maybe the answer will be different. And given that we're very different people living wildly different lives, the answer *will* probably be different."

"Well, if he wants a new dirt bike and you say no because it's not in the budget, it is in my budget. I don't have a budget, Annabel."

"This is definitely part of what I'm talking about. What I'm worried about. Things are going to be different. Parenting isn't about snapping your fingers or throwing money around. It's about being there."

He was quiet for a moment and then nodded. "Agreed. But if I can ease any burdens, I want to. And yes, I want Cody to have extras. I can afford it."

She bit her lip and took a sip of her drink. "It's not the money thing necessarily, though I'm sure that'll come up. It's… I'm not the only parent anymore."

"You worried about that?" he asked. As gently as he could.

She gave a small shrug. "You're his hero."

He stood up and walked the few feet to the leather chair beside hers and sat down. He took her hands in his, which sent surprise skittering across her pretty face.

"Oh, I think *you're* his hero, Annabel. I have no doubt about that."

Her eyes welled with tears, which sent surprise skittering in *him*.

He put a hand on her shoulder, and she swiped under her eyes. "We'll make this work, I promise. There's a huge learning curve for me. There's a lot for you to get used to. Big changes for both of us. But I promise, Annabel—we'll make this work."

She looked up at him. "Okay. I hear the conviction in your voice."

He supposed that was good because he had no idea where the conviction was coming from. Just like he had no idea how to be a father, he had no idea how they'd make this all work. He just knew they had to. And when Logan Winston *had* to do something, he did it.

She stood as if preparing to leave. And if he were honest, he could use a break from the conversation. "Is it hard being back here?" she asked. "You left and never looked back."

"Yeah, it's hard. But I have a child here now. And you're here."

She looked at him, then headed toward the front door. "Me? I've always been here, Logan."

He hadn't meant to add that part about her. He wasn't sure how it even slipped out. She was a very necessary part of all this. His son's mother. A piece of his past in this town was good—not just good, beautiful. When he looked at Annabel, he wasn't reminded of anything hard or harrowing. He just saw a beautiful woman who'd overlooked the rumors and whispers about him eight years ago and gone on a mini adventure with him, taking him out of his life for those three amazing days.

He could forget exploring where things could go now. His relationship to Annabel Dawson was complicated enough; she was his child's mother and he had to be very careful with that. He'd screwed up enough things in his life to know that you didn't mess with the most important.

And right now, Cody Dawson, being that boy's

father—however the hell a person actually did that beyond the word and title—was the most important.

When Annabel got home, her mother had decaf and mini quiches waiting in the kitchen. Her shoulders sagged with relief. What would she do without this wonder woman? Dinah Dawson was always there with her presence and experience and wisdom and love, with coffee and a savory snack. Coming home alone tonight, after all that at Logan's cabin, to a quiet, dark house, not that Annabel ever could because Cody was so young and she'd never leave him alone, would have been hard.

"So how are you two going to handle joint parenthood?" Dinah asked, bringing over a mug of coffee and setting out the cream and sugar.

"We didn't actually get very far in that conversation," she said, wrapping her hands around the mug, the sweetness of the steam a comfort. She took a sip. "He just kept reiterating that he wants to be Cody's father, that he *will* make this work."

"Well, that's certainly what we want to hear," her mother said.

Annabel bit into a tiny quiche. Lorraine, her favorite. "I guess I should try not to worry. He's here now. When he leaves, if the novelty of suddenly being a seven-year-old's father wears off and he's on the road and that becomes the priority, I guess I'll just have to deal with that as it comes up."

"Do you get that feeling from him?" her mom asked. "That Cody will be out of mind, out of sight when Logan's back on the road?"

"Not necessarily. He seems to mean what he says—I think. I just don't know—I don't know *him*."

"Hmm, you do, though," her mother said, sipping her own coffee. "People tend to show you exactly who they are right away, if you're paying attention. That he won your heart for three days tells me a lot about him. Because I know *you*. You're levelheaded, not impulsive, careful. Maybe too careful, even. So if you fell for Logan Winston when his name meant something else around here than it does now, there's good reason."

"But he left," Annabel said. "I certainly wasn't cause to stay. Maybe Cody won't be reason to return, either." Her stomach ached at just the thought.

"Well, that's what's going to be at the heart of the issue, Annabel. *Why* he left. Why he never came back. Not even for his dad's funeral. What drove him out hurt worse than anything else going on his life. Maybe he'll be forced to deal with that while he's here for a week. Especially because he now has a son. He *is* here. That's something. And he was here *before* he knew Cody was his."

Annabel felt herself brighten. "You're right. I hadn't thought of that." She took a sip of her coffee, then realized something. "Wait—his manager arranged all that. Staying at the Wyoming guest ranch where his biggest little fan lives so he can recuperate is all spin. He's here for optics."

"But he *is* here. Something tells me if Logan Winston wants to say no, he says no. And people listen."

Annabel pictured steamroller Savannah and wasn't so sure about that. But still, her mother had a point. Logan was the star. And she already could see that he felt things deeply and thought about them. Like his current situation.

"Tomorrow's gonna be some day," Annabel said. "The three of us are going school supply shopping and then helping Cody label his family tree. Both sides."

She thought of her son asleep upstairs in his room, his arm around his stuffed bull, his poster of his hero, his father, on the wall above his rising and falling chest. Cody had a dad now. His dream, certainly. And Annabel's, if she'd let herself really think about it. When Cody was a toddler, Annabel used to fantasize about Logan coming back to town, finding out they had a son, and that they'd live happily ever after. But reality and single parenthood had soon quashed those fantasies that would keep her up at night.

She'd gone from imagining Logan Winston teaching her son how to ride a horse to working on her budget in his birthday month, when a party and a gift would throw her off course.

She'd taught her son to a ride a horse. And she'd made her budget work. Month after month, year after year.

She'd make this work, too.

"I think we're all headed somewhere good, Annabel." Her mother nodded firmly and popped a mini quiche into her mouth.

It helped that her mom was positive about everything.

I will be also.

Chapter Six

"So I've got some news," Logan said just before 8:00 a.m. the next morning to his phone screen, on which Savannah Walsh's face was currently displayed.

The coffee maker pinged in his kitchen, and he headed in to pour himself a cup. To let his eagle-eyed manager see him pick up the pot of brew with his uninjured wrist, he angled the phone against the cookie jar, which he'd discovered was full of thin, crispy chocolate chip cookies, his favorite.

"Please don't tell me you further injured your wrist," she said, pushing her glasses up on her nose. "Anything else is fine."

He poured his coffee, then added mocha-enhanced creamer. He stood right in front of the phone screen. "How about that I'm someone's father."

She slapped a palm to her forehead, red bangs flying. "Oh good God, Logan. When is she due?"

Logan almost choked on his sip of coffee. "I didn't say I'm *going* to be someone's father—I said that I *am*. She was due seven years ago and I had no idea. I missed every second of this boy's life until yesterday."

"Wait a minute," Savannah said, narrowing her eyes. He could see her mind working, going over the bits of conversation during yesterday's walk from the ranch gate to the petting zoo. *Briefly dated before he left town...* "You're not telling me that your little *fan* is your son. Your actual *son*?"

"Yup, that's what I'm telling you. The feature in the paper brought everything to a head. It's a long story why I didn't know. A short story, really, but complicated. His mother—Annabel—was going to tell me but then we showed up."

"Holy corn dog," Savannah said. "For the first time in my life, I'm speechless. Wait, no I'm not, phew. I'm not even going to make a thing of this, Logan. This is nothing to spin. Nothing to turn into a photo op. This is...big. For you, I mean. Not your public. It's none of their danged business."

"Damn right," he said. He wasn't even surprised that Savannah was putting his privacy first. When it came down to it, his manager cared about him and he knew it.

"The news will get out, though, Logan. Bear Ridge might be a small town but the gossip will spread fast and one post on the ole interweb later… I already put out the story of how you're recuperating at the dude ranch where your biggest little fan lives. The minute it's revealed that he's your long-lost son? The Dawson Ranch is private property but there'll be reporters swarming by the gates and social media blowing up with questions and speculation."

"I'll handle it, Savannah," he said. "With a simple, yes, I am a father, and my family and I need privacy right now. An acknowledgment should help."

"It's bare minimum, but just what the situation requires. And I suppose all the stories and speculation and why did he this, why didn't he that, will come out and you can either address those or not. People will be bothering Annabel, too. Warn her. Cody, too. He'll have reporters shoving phones in his face for sound bites."

Ugh. He hadn't thought of that. He'd have to talk to Annabel about the security at the Dawson Family Guest Ranch, which seemed decent. The only way in was through the gates and past the Welcome Hut, which was always staffed, twenty-four hours a day. But reporters were relentless and would canoe over the river and through heavy brush in the dense woods to get on the property and snap candid photos of the "new instant family."

He'd see. Right now, he had school supplies to shop for.

"Oh, and Logan," Savannah said, and he could swear he could see her eyes getting misty. "Congratulations. On being a father."

He stared at her for a moment, waiting for a snarky follow-up. But she looked absolutely sincere.

"I just hope I don't mess this up," he said. "I don't know what the hell I'm doing."

"Just be yourself," she said. "Clichéd and banal but the truth. Do what feels right to you. That's most of it."

"What's the rest?" he asked.

"Figuring it out," she said. "But you'll be fine. You're not alone there."

True. He had Annabel. She struck him as a great mother.

"You'll be fine," Savannah said. "I know you."

"Appreciate that. Because I'm not so sure."

"I am. You take care of that wrist. No lifting that kid! He's probably fifty pounds. Signing off."

He frowned. He liked the idea of hoisting up Cody in the air and catching him. Walking around the ranch with the boy on his shoulders, like he'd seen dads do with their kids since he was little.

One thing at a time, he told himself. And right now, it was school shopping time. Then the family tree.

You'll be fine, he repeated, Savannah's words trying to find a foothold.

At nine that morning, there was an unusual number of people hanging out at the petting zoo, which Annabel could see from her side living room windows. A heads-up from Daisy had come a little while ago to report that news of Logan's stay was all over social media. Usually the ranch was open to the public for à la carte horseback riding and the petting zoo and wilderness tours, but Daisy had scaled back because of gawkers who were surely buying tickets they probably wouldn't use.

The VIP concierge had gotten in touch with Logan about his needs for the day, and like magic, there was a golf cart, complete with a driver, to take them down along the back route to the parking area to avoid the crowd.

Who knew that going to the general store to buy poster board, construction paper and a couple of glue sticks could turn into such an adventure? Cody, for one. He was sitting next to Logan in the golf cart, gazing at his hero with open adoration and chattering about life as a champion bull rider.

Though now, Logan wasn't just Cody's hero; there was much more to the feelings inside his little chest and body. Logan was his *father*. When Cody had come racing downstairs after waking up, he'd asked if he'd had the best dream of his entire life or if Logan

Winston was really his dad. Annabel assured him it was true, and Cody started jumping up and down. He'd eaten his pancakes and apple slices, barely able to chew with his mouth closed for all the questions about what sons and dads did together and if he and Logan would do those things. Annabel again assured him she was sure they would.

While he's here, she didn't add.

A week from now, Logan would leave and who knew when he'd come back to visit. That would be the new question, she had no doubt. *Mommy, when is Logan coming? Did he say?*

Then again, based on the Logan she'd talked to last night, she had a feeling he'd take the matter very seriously. Draw up his own schedule and give Cody a copy.

En route to the parking area, Cody kept up a running commentary to Logan about everything they passed. She and her son had gone on many hikes together along the river and he knew just about every inch of the ranch. Annabel could tell that even Logan was impressed by Cody's knowledge of the different trees and which berries were edible and which were poison. Logan asked him follow-up questions that Cody could easily answer and again Annabel was surprised by how aware and in tune Logan seemed to be of how to talk to a child.

At the Welcome Hut, they hopped out, Logan

picking up keys to the shiny silver SUV rental that had been dropped off for him this morning.

The color didn't go unnoticed by her.

Don't read into this favorite color nonsense, she told herself. She'd thought about it for a while last night as she'd lain in bed, staring out the window at the bottom of the moon just visible. *You were the girl he'd let get away—the girl he'd gotten away from— and you're a nice memory. You're the girl in the puffy silver coat whom he had three special days with before he finally left Bear Ridge. So suddenly silver became his favorite color. It doesn't mean anything.*

Apparently he hadn't planned on having a vehicle during his recuperation, but given all that had occurred, he'd changed his mind after clearing it with his doctor. Annabel had a car, but it was tiny. Within this five-minute span of "extras" being dropped off, she was getting a glimpse into just how different Logan's life was from hers and Cody's. She wondered just how much Cody's life would change in that regard.

Of course, Logan had also requested a brand-new booster seat for Logan, expertly installed (talk about finger snapping), which Cody had excitedly hopped into. Annabel settled into the passenger seat and buckled her seat belt, so aware of Logan at the wheel, his right thigh, his arm, so close to her that she was full of flashbacks.

The sight of his profile, strong straight nose, the

square jaw, the tousled dark hair bringing her back to the last time she was in a vehicle with Logan Winston. The night before he'd left town. They'd gone to Clover Mountain with a blanket and a picnic basket that he'd filled with purple grapes and a hunk of cheddar cheese and a loaf of French bread. She'd been so surprised by how romantic it all was. In her heart of hearts, she believed it was there, in that shallow cave they'd found in a remote area, that Cody had been conceived. Or quite possibly in the B and B he'd taken her to afterward. But their time in the inn had gotten less romantic as the night had worn on, the call Logan had gotten, which Annabel suspected had been from his dad, upsetting him and causing him to be quiet for a while until he regrouped.

But something about the night had been ruined, talks of hopes and dreams turning to how hard life could be. Then Logan trying to lighten things up, saying how lucky she was to have such a close-knit, supportive family. That was when she'd said that she wanted a big family of her own someday, four or five kids. And that was when *he'd* said he didn't want children.

But because she was eighteen and he was twenty-one, talk of children and family hardly registered. By the time he'd fallen asleep, his hand clasping Annabel's, she'd been wide-awake, wondering what a relationship with Logan Winston would be like. Was he a wild card? Or would he always be the attentive, doting guy he'd been during the past few days? Anything and everything seemed possible. She'd just known that she wanted to be with him. Needed to be with him. She had figured having Logan as her boyfriend would be pretty intense. Her own life had been pretty even-keeled. *I'm up for it*, she'd told him silently. *I'm here for you.*

But of course in the morning, he was gone.

Now, they both kept stealing glances at each other. Was he remembering, too? As they headed down the long road toward the center of town, she could definitely feel tension coming from him. The way he sat straight up. The stiffness of his shoulders. How not-relaxed his hand was on the steering wheel. She wanted to ask him if he was okay, but it was clear he wasn't all that okay—and this wasn't a conversation to have around Cody.

Soon enough they arrived on Main Street, and she realized *that* was the cause of his stiff shoulders and white-knuckle grip on the steering wheel. Bear Ridge. His hometown. Being back here. The line of brick-housed shops along Main Street, the town green across the road, where the majestic town hall, a beautiful stone building for a tiny town, rose up in front of two cannons next to a flagpole. The three schools just visible at the far end of Main Street.

There were a lot of people out and about, sitting at the outdoor tables in front of the coffee place, folks walking dogs, the grocery store parking lot already pretty full at just after nine on a Saturday. Given how Logan felt about the place, he likely didn't notice how cute Bear Ridge had become with all the new shops and their modern signage. The town was small, yes, but not sleepy, and had a Western edge. Lots of shops and businesses had opened in the almost eight years he'd been gone. A yoga shop, a thrift shop very popular with teenagers, a juice bar that also made interesting crepes, and Annabel's favorite, the expanded bakery where she always bought bread for the week even though the grocery store was more affordable. Cody was nuts about the sliced sourdough for his lunch-box sandwiches.

Logan pulled into a spot just a few spaces up from the general store. He looked around and seemed to relax some, as if he'd noticed how much things had changed.

"Bear Ridge," he said, letting out a low whistle.

"You all right?" she whispered, putting a hand on his forearm.

He looked over at her. "I'm okay," he said, giving her hand a pat, which sent unexpected electric pules shooting up her arm. *Interesting*, she thought, trying to keep her expression neutral. "This is about Cody," he added with a smile in the rearview mirror before turning around to face their son. "So listen, Cody. I'm gonna keep my sunglasses on when we go inside just so I'm not recognizable. I want this shopping

trip to be about what you need, not about me signing autographs."

"Everyone will recognize you with sunglasses on,"
Cody said. "You're Logan Winston. Remember how
I knew it was you right away yesterday when you got
out of Savannah's car?"

Huh. That was true. Annabel had been so surprised by the whole arrival that she hadn't thought
much about that. Cody had known his hero *instantly*.

Logan smiled. "What if I wear *two* pairs of sunglasses?"

"Even then," Cody said with a grin.

Cody turned out to be right. The moment they entered the store, Logan's big aviator sunglasses cov-
ering half his face, a teenager shouted "Omigod, it's
Logan Winston!" and a crowd of people rushed over.
A minute later, the store was mobbed with people
running in from Main Street since word had clearly
traveled fast.

Logan sighed and slipped his sunglasses into the
pocket of his Western shirt. "Hi, folks," he called
out with a wave and a smile. "Your warm welcome
means a lot. Thank you. I'm here with my son and
his mom, and we have some shopping to do for a
school project." He smiled again, held up a hand in
another wave, then leaned over the slots of construction paper with great concentration.

Annabel couldn't hold back the gasp. He'd just
announced, to a crowd of people, that Cody was his

child. The crowd had some gasps in it, too. There were photos snapped and soon enough, the throngs of people did step back.

Annabel saw a few people she knew, eyes like saucers, staring at her.

And Cody was beaming up at Logan with hearts in his eyes.

"I didn't know Logan Winston was your dad," a boy called out, his arms full of poster board. His own father was beside him, looking from Annabel to Logan for some of confirmation.

"Yup, he is," Cody said.

Logan put an arm around Cody. "I sure am," he said with a polite smile. With that, Logan bent his head over the poster boards and in a little while, the crowds dispersed. "What color poster do you want, Cody?"

"My new favorite color is silver," Cody said. "Like yours and Mommy's."

Logan smiled. "Silver it is." Logan pulled out the big silver sheet.

Five minutes later, with a pack of multicolored paper and some new glue sticks, they were back outside, where another crowd was waiting. Again Logan thanked them for the warm welcome and then they piled into his SUV.

"Wow, is this what it's like to be you?" Annabel asked as she buckled her seat belt. "All the time?"

Logan nodded. "I don't do much Saturday-morning shopping in general stores, though. When I do go out in public, it's usually for an event. So I gear up for the crowd. Believe me, I appreciate the people that come see me."

"Did you really think people wouldn't recognize you in sunglasses?" Cody asked from the back seat. "I'd know you anywhere. Even in a ninja costume."

Annabel had no doubt.

"Well, I was hoping," Logan told Cody, looking at him in the rearview mirror. "I wanted this shopping trip to be about you. Not me."

"I liked this shopping trip a lot," Cody said, positively beaming.

Logan slid a glance and a smile at Annabel, and she had the strongest urge to reach for his hand and hold it on the console. Of course, she kept her hand to herself.

You're feeling close to him, she realized. *Because of how he handled the crowd. What he said. How he is with Cody. And you.*

Be careful, she warned herself.

Twenty minutes later, they were back at the ranch. Katie in the Welcome Hut let them know there had been a bunch of reporters and two news vans there a little while ago but they finally left when she assured them Logan was not on the property. Apparently, shots of him in town on social media confirmed that and they'd gone racing away in search. Annabel was glad they'd missed all that.

Logan parked and they started walking up the path to Annabel and Cody's cabin, Logan carrying the packages, Cody keeping up a steady stream of chatter about what type of tree to draw or make for the project.

"It's true!" a woman's voice shrieked from a path leading up from the guest cabins. "Logan Winston is here!" A new crowd came running toward them.

Okay, this could get old fast, Annabel thought.

"Are they gonna run me over?" Cody asked, racing behind Logan's legs.

"Nah, they'll stop a good foot away," Logan assured him. "They always do. Key is to stop, smile, give them what they want, which is really just a quick hello and a few selfies, and then bam, we're on our way again."

Annabel would think that would get really tiresome, but Logan seemed fine with it. Maybe he just saw it as such a part of his life that it didn't even register as annoying.

Cody peeked his head out and sure enough, the group of seven, all adults, stopped, big smiles, phones snapping away, some of them turning around in front of Logan to get a selfie with him in the picture.

"Hi, folks," Logan said with an easy smile he must pull out for these times. "I'm here to recuperate and get this wrist—" he held it up "—in fighting shape for my next bull ride in Cheyenne. And to spend some much needed time with my son here," he added, putting an arm around Cody. "Thanks for coming to say hi." He turned slightly, to politely let them know they should move on.

Again Cody beamed up at him.

"Well, let's not crowd the Winston family," a man said, taking off his hat. "You enjoy your day together," he added to the three of them, and he ushered his own group back toward the cabins.

Winston family.

Goose bumps slid up Annabel's spine—in a good way. Once upon a time, back when Cody was an infant and she still thought it possible that Logan would realize he was in love with her and swoop back for her like in *An Officer and a Gentleman*, she'd fantasized that she and Cody were Winstons.

Now, she was the odd man out. Odd woman out.

The goose bumps were replaced by just a chill, and Annabel almost blurted out that she wasn't a Winston, but the guests were halfway down the path toward the cafeteria.

She glanced at Logan as he slung an arm around Cody and started walking again. She narrowed her eyes at him on the sly. He must have hashed this all out with his manager last night or this morning— how to handle the big reveal. Then again, Logan was just wanting to put the most basic information out there to keep the questions and speculation and reporters at bay. In any case, Logan sure knew how to handle his fans. He'd been exactly right about what would happen.

His life was sure different than hers.

Another group was heading inside the petting zoo barn, so the three of them hurried into Annabel's cabin. Cody raced into his room, probably to get his pencil case with his Magic Markers and scissors.

"Phew," Annabel said, shutting the door and locking it. "Good to have some privacy."

"The family tree will be a lot harder on me than any photo-snapping crowd ever could be," Logan whispered.

Ah, she thought, getting it. Of course it would be. His family seemed to be his least favorite subject. And now, it was his son's school project.

All three of them had a lot to get used to when it came to being a family, no matter how on the outside of that Annabel was.

Chapter Seven

Something about Annabel had Logan saying things that he normally wouldn't—like about the family tree. Probably because all this—being a father—was so new and he had no idea what he was doing—or saying. He was trying, though. Being careful with Cody. But the honesty pouring out of him with Annabel since he'd arrived—unexpected. Maybe it was a holdover from how easy she'd been to talk to all those years ago. Muscle memory at work. Or maybe she felt like his lifeline in this new world he found himself in.

Maybe a combo of both.

Cody came running back with his pencil case. "Are you guys ready to start the family tree?" he asked.

"Ready," Logan said, hoping his attempt to rid his

expression of strain had worked. He handed Cody the two bags from the general store.

Cody slid everything out onto the coffee table and sat down on the rug on his knees. His body was practically vibrating with excitement.

Which is why you're gonna get through this. Just say what you know and that you'll find out what you don't. Don't think about anything you say—the names, what they conjure up.

"Wow," Cody said. "Until yesterday, I couldn't have filled out the side of for my dad. Now I can!"

Logan found himself giving the boy's hair something between a ruffle and a caress, then he sat on the sofa, across the coffee table. He sort of centered himself, and so did Annabel when she sat, so they were once again pretty close to each other. Like they'd been in the car. He could smell a light fragrance again, something very appealing. Her long blond hair, out of its ponytail, was half shielding her profile because she was slightly leaning forward, and he had such an urge to move a swatch back behind her ear. To touch her. To see her.

"I'm gonna draw the tree on the green paper," Cody said, pulling Logan's attention away from how pretty Annabel was, how close, and how aware he was of her. "And then paste it onto the poster board. Is that a good idea?"

"Sounds good to me," Annabel said.

Cody looked at Logan.

"Agreed," Logan said.

Logan could feel Annabel tense—slightly—beside him. That she wasn't the sole parent anymore had to be hard on *her*. And he had to remember that. They were both going through some major newness right now.

In about twenty minutes, Cody had the cute, lopsided tree pasted onto the silver board. He studied the example sheets his teacher had provided of how to add the relatives' names.

"Let's start with Mommy's side," Cody said, his tongue sticking out as he concentrated on selecting the perfect color marker. "Mommy, what does this say?" he asked, pointing at the instruction sheet.

Annabel turned the instructions to face her. "Great-grandparents. Those are Grandma's mom and dad. Do you remember their names?"

"Buppy and Guppy," Cody said. "But I forget their last name."

"Hurley," Annabel said.

"Bubby and Guppy Hurley," Logan put in. "I like it."

"Well, their real names are Barbara and Ben," Annabel said. "But they've always been Bubby and Guppy to Cody. And to me when I was very young. Their dream was to retire to the desert and they live in community for over-seventies in Arizona with a cactus out their window. They love it."

"We visit Buppy and Guppy on holidays and their

birthdays," Cody said. "Mommy, can I write down what I call them or do I have to put their real names?"

"Good question," Annabel said. "How about both? Their real names and then in parentheses, Buppy and Guppy."

"Can you help me spell Barbara?" Cody asked, plucking an orange marker from his pencil case.

Annabel did. But Cody wrote the letters too big for the space, so he cut out a new line and this time wrote the letters too close together so they were impossible to read. He put down his marker and frowned. "I'm bad at writing."

"Barbara's a long name," Logan said. "How about you write the letters and imagine a little dot between each. My mother taught me that trick when I was seven."

Annabel tilted her head, and he could tell she was interested in knowing more about his mother. He hadn't talked about her at all during their time together.

Cody got to work, the little tongue out in concentration. "It's working! The *B* and *A* look okay!"

From disappointed to beaming in three seconds. Kids were amazing in that regard. Grudge holders, they weren't.

Cody finished his great-grandparents' names, then got help with spelling the next generation. "I miss Grandpa. He's the one who took me to the rodeo where I first saw you."

"Was he a big fan of the rodeo?" Logan asked.

"Huge fan," Cody said. "He liked all the events. He took me every time you were close by."

Logan was glad he'd had a grandfather like that in his life, even for a short time. Cody would always have those beautiful memories. "He sounds like a terrific grandpa."

Cody nodded. "He was the best. The GOAT of grandpas."

Annabel teared up, but Logan could see the combo of sad and happy. She reached over to smooth Cody's hair, and Logan could feel her love for him emanating from her.

"You're real lucky to have had a grandpa like that," Logan said. *To have all the Dawsons in your camp. You might not have known your dad for the first seven years, but you had such magic in the Dawson clan. Immediate family and extended.*

Cody brightened and got busy writing Dinah Dawson, then his mother's name. Below in a big purple circle, he wrote, "Lots and lots of Dawson cousins."

For chosen family, he wrote "Oinky: goat, and Bucky and Chappy: chickens."

"All done with Mommy's side!" Cody said, looking over his work. The colorful tree was adorable.

Logan cleared this throat, then leaned forward, taking a sip of his coffee. He went through his mother's side first, Cody writing down the names. "And my father's parents, your great-grandparents, were named

Hal and Suzi Winston. They had one son, my father, Everett Winston. And my father had one son, me."

Cody gasped. "And you have one son! Me!"

Logan winced, then caught himself and smiled. "That's right. Who knew there was a Winston family tradition? Well, other than—" He clamped his mouth shut, catching himself there, too.

"Other than what?" Cody asked, head tilted.

"Every Winston male was crazy about pizza," Logan said.

Cody's eyes widened and he looked at his mother and then at Logan. "I love pizza! I'm a true Winston for sure!"

Logan felt that right in his chest. "I can help you spell Hal and Suzi," he said fast, as if he wanted to get this over with.

Ten minutes later, they were up to Logan's parents. Everett and Connie Winston. Logan helped him spell their names, too.

"When will I meet them?" Cody asked.

"Well, they're gone now," Logan said. "Your grandmother Connie was a lovely person. She made incredible cakes. People used to hire her to make cakes for birthday parties."

"I wish they were still here," Cody said. "What can you tell me about them? Did they like the rodeo? What about goats and chickens?"

"My mom liked the rodeo," Logan said. "My dad didn't, though. He liked horse races."

Cody tilted his head. "Your dad didn't like rodeo? How come?"

"I'm not really sure. He loved watching the horses race, though." And lost whatever paycheck he'd managed to get himself as a ranch hand or handyman to it.

"I like horses," Cody said.

Logan nodded. "Me, too. I have a horse named Sand Dune."

Cody grinned. "Will I get to meet him?"

"Her," Logan said. "And definitely. She lives a few hours away. But I'm sure we can make that happen."

He slid a glance over to Annabel, who looked a bit worried all of a sudden.

"Any aunts and uncles or cousins to add to the Winston side of the tree?" she asked as though she wanted to get off that track.

The track where their lives didn't travel the same route. His in Blue Smoke and on the road, all over the west. Hers and Cody's in Bear Ridge.

"No cousins since so many generations were only children," Logan pointed out quickly; he definitely wanted to get off the subject of his father. "It's a small family on my side. And just me."

"And me!" Cody exclaimed.

Again, straight to the heart. Cody was a really sweet kid. Impossible not to adore.

"That's right," Logan said. "And you." He glanced

quickly at Annabel, then looked out the window. "Well," he added fast, standing. "I think you've got my side down. I'll need to head back to my cabin for a phone meeting with Savannah."

"Oh," Cody said, his disappointment plain as could be on his little face.

Logan eyed him. "But maybe after we can go to my favorite pizza place. Toni and Tony's."

"Yay!" Cody exclaimed, then got up and launched himself at Logan, so fiercely that Logan almost fell backward.

He could feel Annabel watching as he bent slightly and wrapped his arms around Cody. She had a compassionate look on her face, as though she understood he needed to decompress.

"See you later, alligator," Cody said, his hazel eyes so happy and bright.

Logan grinned. "In a while, crocodile."

Cody was beaming again.

The simplest, smallest things brought a smile to the child's face.

He didn't want to do anything to take that smile away.

Today had been some day, Logan thought as he watched Annabel tuck in Cody from his spot in the doorway of the boy's bedroom at eight thirty that night. He paid close attention to everything Annabel did, from how she smoothed the blue-and-white-striped comforter over Cody's little chest and kissed him on the forehead to the way she wished him sweet dreams about all his favorite things.

Now it was Logan's turn. And once again, for the third or fourth time that long, special day, he found himself getting choked up.

You've got this, he reminded himself. Because so far, this fatherhood thing was going really well. Cody made it easy, of course. So did Annabel. When he'd left their cabin after working on the school project, he'd flung himself on the chaise on his patio and stared up at the blue sky for a solid half hour, just letting his mind go where it would. He'd expected to be bombarded by thoughts of his father and grandfather, and maybe that last casual "see you later" with his mother when he had no idea he'd been about to lose her forever. But instead, all he thought about was Cody and Annabel.

Cody, so sweet. His child. His son. Maybe Logan hadn't quite wrapped that around his brain yet. Or maybe Cody just really did make it easy.

He hero-worships you like your fans do, he knew full well. The boy had stars in his eyes for not only having a dad but having Logan Winston as that dad. Things wouldn't always be so easy.

But right now they were.

The trip to Toni and Tony's had been very sweet. Cody insisted on trying Logan's favorite toppings, even though Annabel had reminded the boy that he didn't like peppers, raw or sautéed. But nope, he wanted his pizza his father's way, which resulted in a wrinkled-up face after one bite and Annabel forking off the peppers, which Logan added to his own slices. Cody then gobbled up two slices, loving the sausage. When they'd first arrived at the pizzeria, Logan had been surprised by how nostalgic he felt about the place, which hadn't changed a bit. It was a bit off the beaten path, not directly downtown, more on the "wrong side of the tracks," where Logan had grown up. He'd been surrounded by a small mob of diners the moment he'd stepped inside, and he'd shaken hands and taken selfies with fans, the thrilled owners refusing Logan's money and insisting on treating all three of them. The pizza itself had managed to get only better in eight years.

After lunch, Annabel had suggested a stop at a remote playground where hardly anyone ever went because a brand-new playground that catered to both toddlers and big kids had opened up right on the town green. They'd had the old place to themselves, and Cody had raced around for over an hour on the different structures, Logan watching him or pushing him on the tire swing, getting down and dirty in the huge sandbox to build a giant castle with various pails and buckets that had been left behind.

"This is the fun, easy part of being a dad, I see," Logan had whispered to Annabel as Cody climbed the stairs of a tall green slide.

"Except when there's an accident," Annabel had pointed out, telling him about a fall from a seven-foot climbing structure last year and a twisted ankle, resulting in a boot and crutches for six weeks. She'd also mentioned the little arguments that could break out between kids at playgrounds and the occasional adult skulking around *without* a child. Hardly a place for a mom to sit and relax on a bench with a book and her iced coffee while her child had fun. Parents needed to keep an eye and an ear out at all times, it seemed.

After the playground, they'd gone back to the ranch, Annabel calling her cousin Daisy to see if the petting zoo was super busy or if they could go and not have Logan be surrounded. Turned out Annabel had some finger-snapping powers of her own because Daisy had closed the petting zoo for a half hour at the off-time, and the three of them had had a blast feeding the goats pellets from the little machines and watching them hop on and off their logs and go in and out of their little toy houses. Cody had introduced his favorite chickens to Logan and when it was time to go wash up and rest for a while, Cody had said this was one of the greatest days of his whole entire life. They'd gone back to the cabin, and he and Cody had built LEGO towers while Annabel had grilled burgers and baked potatoes—she'd refused any help—and after dinner they'd watched an animated movie.

Except for the part where he'd had to think about his family, today had been one of the best days of Logan's life, too.

Then he'd supervised Cody's bath, which involved Cody playing with a bull rider figurine and a bull with little gray drifts of smoke coming from both nostrils. The sight had almost done him in; he'd realized he was choked up and had had to stand up for a moment and compose himself. Then he'd worried about not watching Cody's every moment in the bath and had sat back down on his knees until he remembered the boy was seven, not two.

Now Annabel moved away and Logan stepped over, sitting on the edge of the bed.

"Thanks for the great day," Logan said, smoothing the comforter over Cody's chest. And swallowing around the sudden lump in his throat. Such a simple gesture but somehow...*big*.

"But you're the one who made it so great," Cody said, eyes heavy and fighting closing. "Even though I still hate peppers, I now know I like sausage on my pizza. I thought I only liked pepperoni." He let out a great big yawn. "Oh, will you tell me again," Cody added, "what you say to the bulls right before the chute opens?"

Logan glanced at the bull wrapped in Cody's arm. "I tell each one the same thing every time. That even though he's not gonna throw me, he's awesome and not to forget it."

Cody grinned. "That really is super nice of you," he managed to say before his eyes closed, his little chest rising and falling in his pj's. He seemed sound asleep.

Annabel smiled. "He'll probably ask you ten more times." She turned around and suddenly covered her face with her hands.

Logan stood and walked over to Annabel. "Hey, what's wrong?"

"It's just…a lot," she said. "Everything, I mean. Today."

"Yeah. A lot. Times a million."

She managed a quarter of a smile and nodded, then glanced at Cody and headed out, Logan following her. She left the door ajar and they went downstairs.

Annabel got them two craft beers and set out a plate of bakery cookies, and they sat down on the sofa, again both kind of in the middle.

He took a swig of his beer and leaned his head back, barely able to believe what his life had become in just days. "Last night when I finally got myself to bed, I kept thinking about all those years ago— seeing you standing on the side of the road next to your car in that silver coat and how I normally wouldn't have taken that route. If I'd gone my usual way, I never would have met you. There'd be no Cody."

"That's impossible for me to imagine. My life without Cody. I'm glad you did go that way."

He looked at her for a moment, then glanced down at his beer. "Around midnight the day I left, I drove halfway back to Bear Ridge," he blurted out. "I was coming back for you." He hadn't meant to say that. He hadn't let himself think about that in eight years—why would he tell her such a thing?

She gasped and was staring at him. "You did? I mean, you were?"

He took another swig of his beer, his hand tight around the bottle. "I had this entire conversation with myself. How I should have asked you to come with me and that maybe you would have. I kept going back and forth about it and then got in my pickup and drove about an hour and a half when I realized I couldn't ask you."

She tilted her head. "Why?"

"Because what kind of life was I going to give you? A guy you knew three days? With no money, no prospects, except a far-fetched dream to get good at bull riding and maybe win some prize money. To have a ranch someday. *Someday* was the big word back then, Annabel. I had nothing."

"You had a lot, actually," she said, then her cheeks kind of flushed. "Your dreams, for one. Which you made come true."

"You're like Savannah—you saw potential in me."

She shook her head. "Actually, I just liked you as you were."

That touched him a little too much, and he found himself leaning closer to her, a hand going to the side of her face, her soft cheek. Right then, she was that girl who'd made him feel special, like he could do anything, even become a competitive bull rider.

He leaned closer still, and the instant his lips touched hers, he felt the electricity of it in every part of his body. She scooted closer, too, deepening the kiss, her light perfume wrapping all around him.

But then she pulled back. "Not a good idea," she whispered. "For a lot of reasons."

"I know," he whispered back, letting his hand linger on her face for just one more second. He knew exactly what those reasons were.

"I know what the number one reason is for me," he said. "But what is it for you?"

She seemed surprised he'd asked—or maybe in that way. "Cody just got you," she said. "I won't do anything to mess that up."

He tilted his head. "What do you mean?"

"Romance ends, Logan. People lose interest. People leave. People fall for others. If we're romantically involved, it'll eventually come to an end. Maybe in a few days when we know each other better as the people we are now and discover we're not compatible. Maybe in a week, when you have to leave. And maybe things don't end well between us. Maybe one of us wants more. There are lots of ways this could go bad. And if it does, if there's friction between us, guess who'll get hurt the worst?"

He sucked in a breath. "Cody."

"Right. I want to protect the relationship between the two of you. That has to be the most important thing here, Logan."

He nodded slowly. She was right. And Logan wasn't good at romantic relationships. At twenty-eight years old, his longest had lasted all of six weeks and that one ended badly. *What do you mean you don't know if we're headed somewhere?* the ex had asked. *I mean, do you have feelings for me or not? What do you mean you don't really know that either?* She'd gotten angry and had huffed off with: *Hope you get thrown in your next competition. Jerk.* Then she stormed back in with tears in her eyes and said she didn't mean that. *But you're still a jerk.*

He certainly never set out to hurt anyone. He'd started being honest from the first date: *You should know, I'm not looking to get serious.*

Sometimes his date would say, *Same here* or *Who says we won't fall madly in love?*

Logan would always respond with, *The most important relationship in my life will always be only eight seconds long.*

Most of his dates smartly walked away after that. A few after tossing their drink at him with *What a cold thing to say.* Or bursting into tears and running off. But a few would claim they were in it for the fun, too, or liked dating a rodeo celebrity. Logan only knew that being honest, and sometimes to the point of being straight-out cold, was the right thing to do.

A chill ran up his spine. He was the guy who was suddenly tasked with the great responsibility of being a boy's father?

He stood, his stomach twisting. "I understand," he said. "That's what I want, too." He headed toward the door, needing the air on the other side. "I can see Cody tomorrow?" No one knew better than Logan that practice was the key to performance. If he wanted to be the father Cody deserved, Logan would need to work at it. Not run from it.

"He has a family birthday party in the morning, but he'll be free after two," Annabel said.

"I'll pick him up at two. We'll have a boys' day out."

"He'll like that," she said.

And it'll keep us away from each other, he could see her thinking.

Thing was, he'd like her to be there, too. Not just because he was so new to fatherhood that he felt more comfortable with her around. But because he just liked being near her.

And he couldn't stop thinking about that kiss.

Chapter Eight

At a few minutes after seven the next morning, Logan sat on a bench just outside the gated playground in Bear Ridge Park, finishing up his coffee and a bacon, egg and cheese sandwich from a food truck. The park wasn't crowded this early—just three little kids and their caregivers in the playground, some dog walkers and joggers, and two guys with fishing poles headed toward the river. Logan stared at the slides and monkey bars and chutes and climbing structures. He had no doubt he'd be bringing Cody here over the next couple of weeks. Maybe even this afternoon, when he was done with the family birthday party.

Logan had been watching the three tots move around the area meant for small kids, their caregivers never farther than an inch away. He still couldn't see himself as someone's father, a dad cheering on a reluctant slider or keeping an eye as a small hand reached for the next monkey bar on the row, five feet up from the ground.

He might not feel like a dad yet, but he was one.

Logan had his sunglasses on less for the bright sunshine or an attempt to be incognito than to keep a distance between himself and…real life. Reality that he was a father. Reality that he was really back here in Bear Ridge—and now had a tie that would mean coming back. Again and again.

He wasn't entirely sure if the chills running up and down his spine were from one or all of those things.

As he looked around the park, though, he was struck by the realization that he had good memories here, too—and not just from three days with Annabel Dawson. Like at the duck pond, where his mother took him every day after school and on weekends to feed the ducks day-old bread, then to this very playground. She'd worked six days a week as a nurse's aide at the Bear Ridge Clinic, an early shift, so she was free in the late afternoons, and off they'd go, always starting on the tire swings where she'd give him great big pushes, though she must have been exhausted from the physical workday. Then they'd sometimes stop for ice cream, and on payday, his favorite pizza place, Toni and Tony's. She'd made those afternoons so wonderful for him that when they got home to his father, whose mood and level of inebriation would dictate how the evening went, he could sometimes just block out his dad—and the arguments. When he hit his early teens, he used to wonder why his mother had stayed with his father— till the day she died. He didn't get it then and he still didn't. She always used to say, *I made a commitment and even though your father is a handful, I do love him.*

Wasn't any wonder to Logan that love was hard for him.

He sighed and lifted his face to the beautiful breezy morning—sunny and fifty-eight degrees, which was helping to clear his head. Besides being bombarded with memories about his family since he'd arrived, last night something else, something much nicer to recall, had slid into his thoughts: unexpectedly kissing Annabel.

He was surprised that he *had* kissed her; he rarely did anything these days without thinking hard about it. Having a beer the night before a competition: will this hurt my chance of winning in the slightest? Maybe. No beer. Signing on as spokesman for a particular company? He'd have Savannah explore every angle of the corporation, whether a brand of cowboy hat or a beverage. Go on a second date with a woman who'd inadvertently dropped hints that she was relationship-minded? Never.

But he'd kissed Annabel Dawson because he *hadn't* thought. He'd only *felt* in that moment and had gone with it. A kiss wouldn't happen again; she'd made certain of that with what she'd said about them needing to protect Cody from a romance between them burning to the ground and causing problems. So that nothing would get in the way of Logan developing and building a relationship with his son.

Logan knew only a few bull riders with families. One, a guy named Lance, had his marriage annulled—well, the ex-wife did—the day after the wedding when rumors that he'd slept with a guest at the reception turned out to be true. The bull rider had told Logan he'd only proposed in the first place because she was pregnant and he wanted to do the right thing by her—and his child—in at least *that* regard if not others. By the time the baby came, the exes despised each other to the point that they were constantly in court over custody issues. *He was three minutes late returning Timmy from his Sunday visitation, so I'd like to revoke visitation. I saw her wheeling Timmy in his stroller without a hat on when it was forty degrees—negligence!*

Logan sure hoped they got it together for that baby's sake. No matter what happened between him and Annabel, Logan had to put Cody first. Given that he'd spent the past seven years putting himself and bull riding before anyone or anything, he wondered how difficult this would be for him. Someone else's needs ahead of his own. Maybe putting your kid first came automatically. Out of a sense of responsibility or love. Not for Lance or his ex, certainly. Or Logan's father. His mother had put herself last, which wasn't good either.

He let out a sigh and lifted his face to the breezy sunshine again, hoping his head would clear a bit like it had when he first sat down. Nope. He took his last sip of coffee when he experienced serious déjà vu.

Heading for the gate to the playground was CJ Clark—his old best friend—and his two little brothers, both boys attempting to climb the chain-link fence and failing with laughter as they dropped to the ground.

No, wait—those two boys, who Logan would say were five or six, couldn't be CJ's brothers. These boys were way too young. Logan was just so used to seeing the three Clarks together. And CJ's brothers had been twelve and fourteen the last time Logan had seen them, which was the day before he'd fled town.

CJ must now have kids of his own, but that was unlikely. With all the responsibility heaped on his shoulders as the oldest sibling of neglectful parents, would he go and have two kids at such a young age? Logan couldn't imagine it.

His former buddy looked just the same. Tall, lanky, thick blond hair. He wore jeans and a navy-blue Henley and work boots. They'd gone to the same school all their lives, but Logan hadn't met CJ till he was fifteen. Logan had always kept to himself, hadn't really talked to anyone unless someone talked to him first, and those were usually the girls. Even back then Logan hadn't been interested in getting seriously involved with anyone, and when he wouldn't commit to being boyfriend-girlfriend, all but the *I'll be the one to win the heart everyone says you don't have* diehards had dumped him after a week.

He and CJ had ended up talking for the first time the night they'd both been at the Bear Ridge PD to bail out their fathers from jail when they were fifteen. They'd hung out together since that night, sometimes barely needing to say a word to each other; their expressions, a look in the eye, a bruise, said it all. They'd understood each other. Both of CJ's parents had been alcoholics and instead of biding his time until he could flee Bear Ridge, CJ had made a promise to his younger brothers to never abandon them, to never leave them with the drunks while he started a new life far, far away. Like Logan had planned. Logan, an only child, had left; CJ had stayed. Logan had sent his friend a text the same as he had to Annabel, that he was leaving, that he couldn't take it anymore. No forwarding number or address. He hadn't spoken to CJ since.

Cold. Just like he'd been accused of, he thought now, as that same rush of shame socked him in the stomach.

And man, did the sight of CJ make him realize how much he'd missed the guy. Eight years ago and now.

"It's Logan Winston!" one of the boys with CJ shouted with glee, a hand on the playground gate before rushing over to Logan's bench, finger jabbing in the air.

CJ turned and stared at Logan, his mouth half dropped open.

Logan stood, tossed his coffee cup and sandwich wrapper in the trash can nearby just as the trio reached him, CJ lagging behind. Logan took off his sunglasses, the two boys, twins he could see now, jumping up and down, telling him they were huge fans of his and they heard he was in town and hoped they'd get to meet him and shake his hand. Logan grinned and stuck out his uninjured wrist, sure he was about get a solid pump, which he did, twice over. The Clark boys told him they had his poster on their bedroom wall and they knew the Bulliminator wouldn't keep him down long—he'd win big in Cheyenne for sure. Logan appreciated their faith.

CJ still hung back a bit. Unsure, Logan could see. He hated that this was how he made his old buddy feel.

"My dad said you two used to be friends," one boy announced. "Is that true?"

Logan glanced at CJ, then back at the boys. "Your dad and I were *best* friends when I lived in Bear Ridge," he said.

"Awesome!" the other boy said.

Logan's answer seemed to put CJ at ease.

CJ put a hand on each boy's head. "These are my sons, fraternal twins Austin and Anders. They'll be six in a few weeks. Guys, I guess I don't need to introduce you to Logan Winston, legend in these parts."

That sounded strange coming out of CJ's mouth. Back when they would hang out together every day, they were both considered troublemakers people expected the worst from. Because of who their fathers were and the low-level trouble they'd get into.

"I'm very happy to meet you two," Logan said with a smile.

Austin turned to his brother. "Bet you can't stay on the tire swing longer than eight seconds with my huge pushes."

"Can, too!" was the response.

Then they ran into the playground.

"Cute kids," Logan said, watching the boys slung belly-first over a dangling tire, laughing and kicking off the ground. He turned to CJ. "I saw you at the rodeo in Harperville one time—with your brothers. About six years ago or so. Charlie was carrying one of those number one foam fingers in silver and it glinted in the sun."

"I've been to a bunch of your events over the years," CJ said. "With my brothers and my sons."

"I wasn't sure how you took me cutting all ties with Bear Ridge," Logan said, laying it out honestly.

Annabel had understood, but that didn't mean CJ had. Leaving, yes. Severing all contact, maybe not.

"I understood," CJ said. "Know what I said when I tried to text you back the day you left and found out your number was no longer in service? I thought, *Good for you, buddy.* Not only did you get out, but you made good pretty fast, too. And I've been with you in that spirit ever since. Every win, I give up a silent *yeah* and no matter what's going on with me or my day, I feel like *I* won something."

Logan pulled CJ into a bear hug—again without thinking. He just did it.

CJ hugged back him, giving him two big claps on the back.

"I know I wasn't the only one you left behind," CJ said. "You'd just started seeing someone you said you really liked. I assume it has something to do with the son no one knew you had? Everyone's speculating on the details of that but no one knows anything."

"*I* didn't know either until the other day," Logan said. "When I left Bear Ridge, I had no idea Annabel was pregnant. She didn't know then, of course. When she found out, I wasn't reachable. And when I was, things seemed complicated."

"Yeah, I bet," CJ said. "For reasons only those close to you would understand."

Logan appreciated that comment so much he wanted to pull CJ into another bear hug.

"I have to say, I'm surprised you became a dad

yourself so young," Logan said. "You had to raise your brothers since when—age six yourself?"

"You know, there were times when I'd be angry at my situation, that I couldn't leave like you did. But I love my brothers—making sure they were all right was the most important thing to me, more important than freedom or getting my own place or leaving Bear Ridge. And when I met my wife, having kids of our own just felt right even though we were twenty-two when the twins were born. Being a father figure is what I knew and what I was probably best at. I love being a dad."

"Why?" Logan asked. At his friend's raised eyebrow, Logan added, "I mean, I understand that you love your sons. But why do you love being a father? The whole concept is probably the only thing I'm scared of."

CJ looked at him for a moment, then at his boys, climbing on the jungle gym, one of them landing with a little thud on the wood chips below and climbing right back on. "I loved my parents, even though they were hard to love, right? Being forced to take care of them sucked, as you know. Having to take care of brothers was completely different—they were *easy* to love and I wanted to make things all right for them. I wanted to take care of them. That's what fatherhood feels like. I love my sons and I want to be everything they need. They're everything *I* need."

"What do you mean, everything you need?" Logan asked.

"Everything about the boys trying to push each other off the jungle gym, laughing their heads off, shouting at top volume, they make waking up in the morning that much more meaningful. When I look at them, I feel...complete. I feel that way when I look at my wife, too."

"Huh," Logan said, not really getting it. Complete? Had Logan ever felt complete?

"I suppose bull riding makes you feel that," CJ added. "It's what allows you to be a champion. The way I feel about my boys allows me to be a champion dad. I'd accept a gold medal for it."

Logan stared at CJ, trying to understand. Then he looked over at the twins. They were lucky kids, that was the only thing Logan did understand about this entire conversation.

Complete. He thought about himself riding a bull, holding on. Winning the prize. Did he feel *complete* then? He couldn't say that was the feeling. He always felt proud. Happy, for sure.

Logan had a lot in common with CJ—and then so little. His friend had worked at the same ranch Logan had as a teenager. CJ had loved being a cowboy just like Logan had, but he'd never been interested in competing in rodeo. Then again, his tie was to family and Bear Ridge whereas Logan's burning need had been to cut his last remaining family tie and get the hell out of town. It was no wonder he couldn't really get what CJ meant.

But what if *that* meant Logan would be doing Cody Dawson a disservice? He wanted to be what Cody needed.

He suddenly felt his friend's gaze on him. "Big changes take time, Logan. You just met your son. I guess my one piece of advice is for you to be the father you wished you had."

"So do the opposite of everything Everett Winston did? That would probably be second nature. I'm not like him."

"I don't mean do the opposite," CJ said. "I mean just what I said—be the father you wished you had."

Okay, now he didn't get *that*. Didn't Logan wish his entire childhood that his father would have done the opposite of everything he did? Not drink to the point he came home stumbling and sometimes passed out on the lawn. Not gambled his paycheck away. Not gotten into fights in bars in town. Not made his mother cry all the time.

Logan stared up at the sky for a moment, not wanting to think about any of this.

This conversation was making his gut twist. "Well, congratulations on everything—settling down, being married, the twins. Having everything you want. You still a cowboy?"

"I'm a foreman at the Three Elk Ranch, you know that small place run by the Garroway sisters? Nice-sized cabin comes with the job, so it's a good situation. And the sisters—twins themselves—fuss over the twins like you wouldn't believe."

"What are your brothers up to?" Logan asked.

"Charlie's at the University of Utah studying finance. And you might remember Dean only ever wanted to become a chef. He's working at a fancy Italian restaurant in Brewer. They're both happy."

"And your parents?" Logan asked, bracing himself.

"Gone. Car accident six years ago—my dad's fault."

Logan winced. He understood that to mean his father had been drunk behind the wheel. "My dad's gone, too. Last year."

"I know," CJ said. "I understood when you didn't come back for the funeral. Your dad always said when he went, he didn't want some fussy event, just toss his ashes in the river where he liked to fish."

"My father never caught a fish in his life. Always too drunk."

CJ nodded only the way someone who got it could and would.

"I need to know how to be a father of a seven-year-old—fast," Logan said. "Got tips?"

CJ grinned and slung an arm around Logan's shoulder. "Tons," he said. "A morning at the playground can teach you half of what you need to know."

"What about the other half?" Logan asked.

CJ laughed. "Time. Being there. Effort. Love. Compassion. Commitment. Having your heart run around outside your body—I forgot who said that."

Oh, is that all? Logan thought, swallowing around the lump in his throat.

After singing "Happy Birthday" to Chloe, newly two-year-old daughter of Annabel's cousin Rex and his wife, Maisey, Annabel slipped away to the far end of the backyard of the ranch's main house with Maisey and Daisy. At the start of the party, Daisy's three-year-old, Tony, announced at the top of his lungs, "My mom's name is Daisy and my aunt's name is Maisey. Daisy and Maisey! Maisey and Daisy!" The twenty-two mini guests hooted and shouted Daisy and Maisey at least five times until Daisy's husband, Harrison, smartly distracted them by making balloon animals, a secret gift of his.

The women settled in three Adirondack chairs with their slices of red velvet cake and lemonade while a magic show was entertaining the little guests for the next thirty minutes. Cody was sitting between little Tony and Chloe on her father's lap.

Annabel could use some girl talk. She'd always been close to Daisy, and she and Maisey had become good friends when Annabel was hired at the ranch six years ago and Cody attended the ranch day care, which Maisey ran. She'd called both women with the basics of the Logan-Cody situation—and the Logan-Annabel past—so they'd hear it from her and not from others, though of course by now, just about everyone knew that Cody Dawson was Logan Winston's son.

"Rex is a little starstruck knowing that Logan Winston is actually staying at the ranch," Maisey said, taking a bite of the delicious cake. "He keeps trying to come up with excuses to meet him but then decides they're not good enough excuses." Annabel knew that her cousin Rex and his brother Ford, who took Cody to all the local rodeos, were big fans of Logan's.

Daisy laughed and tucked a swath of her long blond hair behind her ear. "Harrison met him yesterday on the path by the river. They were about to pass each other by with nods when Tony called out, 'What's that?' and pointed to Logan's wrist brace. Harrison said Logan was really friendly and told Tony all about how a bull threw him. Tony asked if he was mad at the bull, and Logan said, 'Nope, just like it's my job to stay on the bull, it's his job to get me off him.'"

Annabel smiled. She could hear him saying that. Which made her realize she was really getting to know him.

And like him all over again.

"He sounds very kid oriented, which is great for Cody," Maisey said. "How's all that going? I nosily ask."

"So far, great," Annabel said. "But that's to be expected, right? Logan's here recuperating, kind of a captive new dad. And Cody is very easy to be with. But what happens days from now when Logan returns to his life?"

"Isn't Cody a big part of that life now, though?" Daisy asked.

Annabel took a quick bite of cake. "Logan does seem very serious about his new role. I guess we'll just have to see." She bit her lip. She'd never been a "go with the flow" type person and wished she had a magical crystal ball.

"Maybe he'll turn Bear Ridge into his home base and live here, going out on the road only when necessary," Maisey said.

Annabel sipped her lemonade. "I don't know. Bear Ridge doesn't hold good memories for him. And I keep coming back to what he said he right before he left Bear Ridge—and me. That he never wanted kids. But maybe that's unfair. When we were explaining to Cody about why I never told him who his father was, Logan pointed out that he may have felt that way before he knew he had a child but not anymore."

Daisy put down her fork. "He said that? And to Cody? Well, that is big. That's commitment right there. He's saying the past doesn't matter, only the *present*."

Annabel hoped that was true. It seemed to be.

Thing was, she was part of the past and only indirectly part of that present. She leaned forward and then looked left and right to make sure no one was listening, though they were a reasonable distance from the magic show.

"He kissed me last night," she whispered. "We were talking about why he left town—and me— and he said he felt like he had nothing to offer me then, that he'd just drag me down. And when I told him that he had his dreams, he said I was one of the rare few back then, like his manager, who saw his potential. I told him that I actually liked him just as he *was*, and that's when he kissed me."

"Ooh," Maisey said. "You're special to him."

Annabel pushed her cake around her plate. "I don't know about that." She thought about him telling her he'd come back for her, that he got halfway before turning back around. She was special to him to a point. But she had a feeling there would always be a turnaround point with Logan. He'd only get so far before he continued on his path.

"And it sounds like the past still has a grip on him," Daisy said.

Annabel nodded. "It absolutely does. But less me than Bear Ridge itself. It's hard for him to be here. Bad memories all around."

"Not the ones with you in them," Daisy pointed out.

"And there *will* be more kisses," Maisey added.

"No matter what the two of you say. Been there, done that."

"Right?" Daisy said with a grin.

Annabel couldn't contain the smile that brought. Both Daisy and Maisey had tried to stop the bullet train of romance when their Mr. Rights had come along. Daisy had been nine months pregnant and a runaway bride when she'd met Harrison—who'd ended up delivering her newborn on the side of the road. And Maisey had been tracked down by a former US Marshal who'd found the fifteen-year-old message in the bottle, a letter to Santa, that she'd written as a foster child about her wish for a family. But love was stronger than their guarded hearts, and now they both had great marriages and happy families.

Could there be a second chance for her and Logan? When it meant they could be a family? How could she not at least try?

Because there was a lot to lose, she reminded herself.

"Who will volunteer to disappear into thin air and then reappear a moment later?" the magician was asking from his small stage.

A chorus of "Meeeee" and raised hands answered him, including Cody, who was chosen.

What Annabel needed was a little magic herself.

Chapter Nine

Just after two o'clock that afternoon, Logan and Cody were on their way to the very playground where he'd run into CJ Clark and his sons.

He glanced at Cody in the rearview mirror, buckled into his booster seat, flying his cowboy figurine through the air. Time to put all he'd learned from CJ into practice. His head was full of his old friend's advice and Logan hoped he didn't get any of it wrong—or mixed up.

When he'd picked up Cody from his and Annabel's cabin just a few minutes ago, his first thought when she opened the door was how badly he wanted to kiss her again. How physically attracted to her he was. He'd also been aware that he wanted her to join them on their outing—and that had nothing to do with lust and everything to do with wanting to be in her company. Wanting her near.

Because he still had feelings for her? Or so he'd have backup if he messed up with Cody and handled something wrong?

Probably both. But today was a boys' day out and at least he had a little more confidence in himself to be on his own with a seven-year-old now that he had CJ's tips tucked away.

The problem was that CJ couldn't be very specific, and Logan had specific questions. Like, let's say Cody falls off the jungle gym and starts crying. Does he run over and kneel down and scoop him up into a hug, console him? Does he tell him that's just a little scrape on his knee and that he's fine and give his hair a ruffle?

CJ hadn't been able to answer that the way Logan wanted. With a definitive: *do this*. CJ had said Logan should do what felt right in the moment and that he'd only know what that was when and if it came up. He'd know the difference between a hard fall and painful injury versus disappointed wailing that he'd fallen and that he really was fine. Logan wasn't so sure he would.

And when Logan asked CJ how to respond if Cody asked a question he had no answer to, CJ chuckled and had said, *Old buddy, take it moment by moment, day by day. No one has these answers. Only you will when you're in the thick of it. Just go with it and do your thing.*

Logan's *thing* was hanging to a bucking bull for eight seconds, signing autographs, depositing big checks into his bank account—actually, Savannah handled that—and living the good life after working two jobs for a few years when he was coming up to pay those early competition fees and the health insurance premiums since he was required to prove he could cover very costly trips to the hospital.

But now his thing involved being someone's father. This living, breathing, walking, talking bundle of energy and heart. And Logan was all too aware what he meant to Cody. As his hero, as the father he'd just discovered he had. He had to be very careful how he spoke to the boy, how he acted.

But tiptoeing required keeping things on the surface. How were they supposed to develop a real relationship if he was being so danged careful with everything he said and did?

He'd asked CJ that, too. Again he'd gotten a chuckle and *Just be yourself. Do what feels right. You've got this.*

He wasn't so sure he did.

He'd thought if he just did the opposite of what his father would do in any situation, that he'd get it right. But CJ had said it wasn't about doing the opposite. That he just had to be the father he wished he'd had.

"Yay, we're here!" Cody exclaimed from the back seat.

Cody's excited voice shook him out of his scary

thought. He turned into the parking lot of the Bear Ridge park. The playground wasn't too crowded and there were a few kids who looked to be around Cody's age.

Cody undid his seat belt and flew out of the car, running around to Logan's side. When Logan stepped out, Cody grabbed his hand and said, "C'mon, I'll show you my favorite slide. We're not allowed to climb up the slide but if no one's around, I do."

Okay, that one seemed easy. Cody was *announcing* he was going to break a rule. Climbing back up a slide, holding on the sides, your sneakers making squeaky grips on the smooth surface, was every kid's favorite thing to do at the playground. He'd let that go. If someone was at the top of the slide, waiting to come down, then he'd tell Cody he should get off.

Easy peasy.

Right.

"It's Logan Winston!" someone shouted, and a bunch of people started heading in their direction.

Dagnabbit. He just wanted to be here with Cody. Hopefully in a day or two, his fans would be used to seeing him around and he wouldn't create a fuss everywhere he went.

"Hey, folks," Logan said, taking off his sunglasses. "Thanks for the warm welcome. I'm here to spend some quality time with my son. Thanks for saying hi." He gave a warm smile, and then turned to Cody, who was beaming at him, and then scrambled up the slide. The crowd stayed put for about thirty seconds, then moved along.

"Guess what today is?" Cody asked when he reached the bottom of the slide.

"Sunday," Logan said.

Cody shook his head. "Not just Sunday. Something else!"

"Hmm, is it pick whatever ice cream cone you want at Bear Ridge Lickety-Split?" Logan asked.

Cody's face brightened even more, if that was possible. "I think it should be! But that's not what today really is!" As a boy appeared at the top of the slide, Cody ran around to the stairs and climbed up. Once the boy had his turn, Cody called, "Here I come!" And pushed off.

Logan headed around to the front of the slide to watch Cody come down. He had a flash of memory of being here with his mother, Connie Winston waiting for him at the bottom of the slide just like he was doing now. When he was very little, he could remember her opening her arms wide to catch him in a hug.

He wondered if Cody was too big for that. Or too old, really. But *seven* seemed so young.

This was exactly the kind of thing he wasn't sure about.

Logan opted for simply being there, at the bottom of the slide, in a kneeling position so he could give Cody a high five, which he did.

"I'll tell you what today is," Cody said, rushing

off to the jungle gym. Logan followed. As he started to climb up, hanging upside down on the metal bars that spanned a two-foot gap, he said, "It's my half birthday! I'm seven and a half today!"

Logan grinned. He well remembered what a big deal half birthdays felt like when he was young. "Happy seven and a half birthday!" he said.

Cody grinned that adorable I'm-missing-my-two-front-teeth smile and continued scampering on the monkey bars, catching each one.

Logan had missed every one of Cody's birthdays. The first and the last and every one in between. That would never happen again.

Cody jumped down.

"I'm sorry I missed your first seven birthdays, Cody," Logan said. "I want to make that up to you. How about if you make a list of seven birthday wishes, and I'll make them all come true."

Cody's mouth dropped open. "No way. Really?"

"Yup," Logan said. "Seven birthday wishes. I owe you."

Cody jumped up and down. "Wow! Okay. I'm gonna think about what I want." He ran over to the steep red slide and climbed up the stairs.

Logan moved over to the front and stood to the side. He could imagine the list. A new mountain bike. Front-row seats to the Cheyenne Rodeo. The LEGO set of his dreams.

He felt good about this. Seven gifts wouldn't make

up for seven missed birthdays, but they would stand for something: an acknowledgment that something very important had gone uncelebrated. Cody's birth.

As he watched the boy slide down, his hands waving high in the air, he realized he'd like to know about the day Cody was born. How it went. What it was like. If her mother had been with her in the delivery room.

Eighteen and delivering a baby, the child's father not in the picture.

He owed Annabel, too. That was for damned sure.

How he'd make it up to her was harder to figure out, though.

It was now almost 8:00 p.m. and Logan still hadn't brought Cody home. Not that they'd agreed on a time, now that she thought about it. But she'd figured their boys' day out would be a three-hour thing max, and instead it was going on *six* hours.

But Annabel *had* been receiving texts from Logan all day and into evening. Just about every half hour, sometimes a few texts an hour, Logan would mention where they were and something funny that Cody did or said and include a photo of their son.

Their son. That was one of the few times she'd thought about Cody in that way. *Theirs.*

Probably because Logan had been in touch so often that day, making her feel part of his and Cody's boys' day out—and certainly making her feel comfortable with Cody's long absence. Her son wasn't off on a day's trip to the rodeo with his police officer cousins; he was with his *father*.

Annabel wondered if Logan knew how this was affecting her, if he figured she'd be unsettled about Cody being away from her for such a long stretch and so therefore kept her in the loop. Or if this was simply how Logan was. A sharer, open, thoughtful. Maybe a combination of both.

Her phone pinged with a text and Annabel grabbed her cell from the kitchen counter next to the coffee maker. She'd had way too much coffee today.

It was from Logan.

Spent the last of the daylight walking along the river right here on the ranch. Headed up to your cabin now. See you in a few.

She bit her lip as she felt her heart actually move in her chest. She was touched, she realized. By the constant texts. By how special Logan was making this day for Cody.

Because having a son, a child, was a novelty? she wondered. Something he'd get accustomed to and then things would be different? Different *how*, was the question.

She was driving herself crazy—and getting way ahead of herself. She had to take this day by day, which she assumed was what Logan was doing.

There was a knock on the door, which sounded

more like Logan than Cody's tapping knuckles. She hurried over to unlock and let them in. The moment the door opened, Cody sprang inside, almost knocking her over with the force of his hug.

"I had the best day, Mommy! I can't even remember everything we did so I'm gonna go write it all down before bed." With that he flew up the stairs, then in two seconds, came back down. "And guess what? You'll never guess so I'll tell you. Logan said that because he missed my first seven birthdays, I can make him a list of seven birthday wishes and he'll make them come true! I'm going to make my list after I write down everything we did today. Oh, and I caught a frog! I let it go, though." He ran back up the stairs, his pounding feet, even in just socks, racing along the upstairs hallway.

He what? she thought, staring at Logan.

While she was trying to process what Cody had said about Logan granting him seven birthday wishes, Logan had a very happy expression on his handsome face. He'd had a good day, that was obvious. A good time. Nothing had gone wrong.

"I'm going to start Cody's bath, then I'll be back down," she said. "We need to talk."

His happy expression dimmed and she immediately felt bad.

"Something wrong?" he prompted.

"I'm just a little worried about the birthday promises," she said. "But let me get Cody's bedtime routine going, then we'll talk."

He looked at her, confusion on his handsome face. "Okay."

She hurried upstairs. Cody was at his desk, tongue out in concentration, writing his list of what he and Logan had done today.

"First we went to the playground," Cody said, asking for help in spelling *playground*. "Then we got ice cream. I got a chocolate and vanilla swirl cone with all different-colored sprinkles." He wrote down ice cream, spelling it spectacularly wrong, which made her smile. He put down his pencil with an, "Ugh. It takes so long to write stuff down." He turned to her, his smile back, lighting up his entire face. "Then we drove to my school and I showed him around the outside of the building. Then we went to Toni and Tony's for pizza for dinner. Then we came back to the ranch and walked along the river and he taught me how to skip stones. I can do it now, well, not every time. And then I caught a frog right in my hands. It was brownish-green. I let it go back to its family."

"That was nice of you," she said, her heart squeezing. "Sounds like an amazing day."

"Logan isn't just the GOAT of bull riders, Mommy. He's the GOAT of dads."

She forced herself not to gasp. "I'm so glad you had a great time with Logan." He turned and jumped into her arms, holding tight. She could see he was overwhelmed—in a very good way—and exhausted from the big day. "I'm gonna go run your bubble bath. Why don't you change into your bathrobe and drop your clothes in the hamper."

"K, Mommy," he said with a yawn.

She went into the bathroom and drew the bath, squeezing in the scented bubbles. Then she went back into Cody's bedroom. He was already in his blue bathrobe with the bull ears hood, a gift from his grammy last year. She walked him into the bathroom and he got in with his cowboy figurine. "Do you believe that Logan is making seven of my birthday wishes come true? Should I ask for birthday wishes from each age I was or just whatever I want?"

She couldn't help the smile even though she was not comfortable with this wish-granting stuff. "I think you should decide."

He grinned and dunked under the soapy water. Annabel grabbed the shampoo and gave his hair a lather, then used the handheld sprayer to rinse. He stood and she rinsed him all over, then he stepped out onto the fluffy bath mat and she handed him a towel, then his bathrobe.

He smelled heavenly. All fresh and clean and like aloe and honey.

"Why don't you change into your pj's and I'll ask Logan to come up to say good-night, too?"

"Yay!" he said, and hurried into his room.

She let out a breath, a worried one, then went back

downstairs. Logan was in the living room, leaned way back against the couch cushions, staring up at the ceiling. Probably wondering why she'd have a problem with his birthday wish granting. Seven years' worth.

"Say good-night to Cody?" she asked. "He's out of his bath and ready to be tucked in."

He popped up. "Definitely," he said, taking the stairs two at a time.

She followed him but remained to the side of the doorway.

"I had a great day with you today, Cody," she heard Logan say. "Thank you. You're making my learning curve about being a dad really easy."

"What's a learning curve?" Cody asked.

"Well, since I'm new at being a dad, I have a lot to learn. But you're such a great kid, you make being a dad seem really fun and easy."

One day on his own with Cody? Of course it was fun and easy. What about when it wasn't, though? Then what? He'd realize being a father wasn't all little frogs and ice cream and wish-granting and they'd hear from him every few months? Holidays and birthdays?

"I can't wait to make my birthday list," Cody said, and she heard him let out a big yawn.

"Me, too," Logan said. "I'll talk to your mom about getting together tomorrow. Maybe the three of us can do something together."

"That sounds good to me," Cody said, yawning again.

"There, all tucked in," Logan said. "Night. See you tomorrow."

"Night, Logan Winston," Cody said.

He stepped out in the hall, seeming surprised to see her right there. "He's so tired."

She nodded. "I'll go say good-night and meet you downstairs." She headed in and when she went to sit on the edge of Cody's bed, she saw that he was already asleep, his little chest rising and falling, his arm around his stuffed bull.

"Good night, precious boy," she whispered, and leaned over to kiss his cheek.

She watched him for a moment, then turned off the light and left the room, closing the door.

She stopped in the center of the short hallway, giving herself a minute. It wasn't the first time Cody had fallen asleep before she could say good-night. And he'd been tucked in by others before, like by his grandmother or her cousins if they were babysitting for her. But Logan had gotten to say good-night and do the tucking in and it just felt…strange.

Everything about this was just so new, so different. Her life, their lives, had changed.

She went downstairs and found him in the kitchen, sitting at the table and staring out at the woods, the moonlight casting a glow on the trees, which were in full bloom now. He turned and smiled at her, stealing her breath for a second. She could just stand there and look at him for hours.

"We should talk," she said, lifting her chin. *Stop being so defensive*, she told herself. *Just tell him what's bothering you.*

He gave her something of a smile. "I'm listening."

"About the birthday wishes," she began, walking to the far end of the room in front of the side door. Logan stood and followed her, leaning against the wall across from her.

"Right," he said, slightly tilting his head as if still trying to figure out why that was an issue. "He mentioned that today was his half birthday and it struck me that I missed the first seven. I missed so much, Annabel. I want to make up the seven birthdays I wasn't here for."

"By granting him wishes for each one?"

"Yes. Whatever he wants. Birthdays are a big deal to kids."

"Well, I'm sure his list will have regular birthday kid stuff on it like a new bike. But he'll mainly ask for *experiences*."

"Experiences?" he repeated, his blue gaze laser-sharp on her.

"He'll want to do things with you. Go places. Be with you."

"Well, that's fine. I want that, too. We have several days left together and I have nothing else on the agenda." He held up his braced wrist.

"He may ask for things you can't give him. Or won't feel comfortable doing."

"Like what?"

"Like having you move to Bear Ridge. Like having you move into our cabin."

Logan's eyes widened. "Ah."

"Like that days from now, when you go to Cheyenne, you come right back. I can see that being on his list."

"Oh man," he said, looking down and shaking his head. "I'm hardly the GOAT of dads, after all. I thought this was an amazing day but I screwed up bad right in the beginning."

"You meant well, obviously," she said. "But his list might have things on it you can't promise or possibly deliver on. I'm just afraid to think of him getting hurt. Disappointed. Right now he's a novelty and—"

"Whoa," he interrupted. "A novelty? Is that what you think Cody is to me?"

"I wouldn't possibly know, Logan," she said. "I don't know you."

"I'm the same person you fell in love with during those three days," he said, then looked kind of shocked, as though he couldn't believe he'd actually said that. "Just older, wiser and yes, richer."

"Who said I was in love?" she shot back, feeling like this conversation was getting away from her.

"Well, I was," he said, realizing as he'd said it that it was true. "So I thought maybe you were."

She gasped, staring at him. "You loved me?"

He nodded, looking right into her eyes, his expression sincere. "Yeah."

I came back for you that night. Well, halfway before I turned around... He had loved her. He'd made a choice to let her go, to save himself and maybe even her so that he wouldn't, as he'd said, drag her down, and it had to have hurt.

"Before every competition," he said, "I'd think of you, picture your face, the way you believed in me, and I knew I'd stay on for eight seconds. You were like my good-luck charm."

Oh, Logan, she thought, her heart cracking open. "I loved you, too," she whispered and walked right into him, wrapping her arms around his neck. One hand tipped up her chin and then he kissed her. Hard.

What the hell are you doing? she asked herself, but it was too late to take it back. She wanted this. Needed this.

He walked her against the wall, every part of his body flush with hers until he was pressed even closer, the wall at her back giving them no leeway, no escape from the delicious sensations building in her core. He deepened the kiss and she met him with everything she had, wrapping her own arms around him, moving her hands across his shoulders, down his back, up the front of his Henley shirt to slide to his chest.

She heard him groan. And then she stopped thinking about anything but how this felt.

"Tell me Cody is a very heavy sleeper," he whispered, then kissed her along her neck.

She barely managed to nod, his lips now on her collarbone and dropping lower. "Herd of bulls stampeding wouldn't wake him."

He pulled away and looked at her as if searching her eyes, giving her the chance to catch her breath and tell him again that this was a bad idea. But she wasn't sure anymore. Bad idea. Good idea. Should they try to pick up where they'd left off, but as these new people they were, in this new situation? Or should they be careful, like Annabel had originally thought, for Cody's sake?

What if they could grow into a family, though? That would be the ultimate. Cody could have both his parents together…and Annabel would have what she'd once hoped for, dreamed of, until reality had made it clear it wasn't happening.

It was sort of happening right now.

Logan was back.

He had all the facts.

She wasn't sure *she* did—like…what were his intentions? He likely didn't know himself—but at this moment, his hand on her cheek, the way he was looking at her, with pure unadulterated desire in his gaze, she just knew with certainty that she wanted him right back.

Besides, you're getting ahead of yourself again, she thought, as she took his hand and led him upstairs to her room. This was all part of figuring things out.

When was the last time she'd been naked with a man? She couldn't even remember.

Once inside, she shut the door with her foot and he kissed her over to the bed, where they fell onto it, too busy kissing, their hands exploring under each other's shirts, to say a word.

He lay propped on top of her, his lips fused to her, his hands everywhere. He lifted her T-shirt and opened his eyes, his gaze taking in her lacy white demi-cup bra. He kissed the mounds of her breasts, then unhooked the bra and flung it aside, his mouth taking in each nipple, his fingers lightly pressing. She writhed beneath him, wanting her yoga pants off—now.

Wanting him naked.

She pulled off the Henley, her hands all over his stomach and chest, drawing him down closer. She kissed him hard and passionately and then she finally felt him nudging down the yoga pants. Too slow—she couldn't take it. She peeled them off, then reached for his belt buckle, then the snap of his jeans.

And finally, they were naked. His lips trailed down her breasts, down her stomach, his fingers exploring between her legs, and Annabel writhed again, arching her back, barely able to take the strains of pure sensation that rocked her. He kissed his way back up and then she managed to flip him onto his back.

She straddled him, and now it was her turn to kiss every bit of his body, his hard, muscled chest, the light line of hair straight in the center of his belly. She gripped his erection, and he groaned, her hand moving up and down. His eyes were closed but then he opened them and they locked gazes, but she was half out of her mind with desire for him.

He reached around for his jeans where they'd landed half off the bed and found his wallet, rummaging through until he found what he was looking for. A condom. He held it up. "This thing failed us once, but it's all I have."

"I've been on birth control since Cody was born," she said. "But we should still use the condom," she whispered.

He tore off the top of the little packet and then in moments, they were once again one, moving in passionate sync, Annabel breathing hard, low moans escaping her, her nails slightly digging into his strong back. She loved every time he groaned.

All her memories from her three days with Logan Winston came rushing over her. Except now, he wasn't an unsure-of-himself twenty-one-year-old. And if she'd thought sex with him then was incredible...

He pulled up a bit and she opened her eyes to find

him looking into them. "You are so beautiful," he said, stroking her hair and gazing at her so tenderly, with such emotion.

Don't make me fall in love with you, she thought, but then he was moving against her—hard and fast—again, and all thought left her.

Chapter Ten

Logan woke up in the middle of the night, a glance at Annabel's alarm clock on her bedside table letting him know it was close to 3:00 a.m.

She stirred next to him. He was spooned against her, his body wrapped around hers. He wished he could see her beautiful face. Then he got his wish because she turned around to face him with a sexy smile.

"Hmm," she said, snuggling closer, her eyes closed.

"I know," he whispered. He couldn't possibly get close enough to her. *This* was the feeling he'd missed, what he'd been waiting to find in the dates and short-term relationships he'd had over the years. "I shouldn't be here when Cody wakes up, right?" he asked. "I mean, does he wake up at the crack of the dawn and will he come running in here?"

She opened her eyes. "Yes on both counts. And to the first thing you said, I don't think we should set up any expectations for him, like that we're back together. As a couple. Unless we agree that's what we are—or where we're headed."

She was looking right at him. Waiting for him to respond to that.

"I'm going to be honest, Annabel. Like you said the first time we kissed, everything about you and me is complicated. It's clear I have feelings for you. That I want you. That's very clear." He gave her something of a smile, and she gave him something of one back. "But when does romance ever work out? What if this doesn't work out? How will that affect Cody? If there's hurt feelings and tension between us? How will that carry over into how we act when we have to see each other, when I come pick up or return Cody. And are we supposed to keep this re-kindling of our old flame from him?" He shook his head. "I don't have any answers."

"Me either," she said, biting her lip.

"I just know there's something really good between us," he said.

"Agreed," she said.

"But I *do* have to leave soon, as you know. I've got the competition in Cheyenne, which is four hours from here, and then the *New York Times* is actually doing a story on me for their Sunday magazine if you can believe that. The reporter and videographer will be trailing me for a week as I prepare for the US championships in August—practicing every day at the Blue Smoke arena, the local appearances. Savannah's thinking of using that to get a documentary about me going, shopping it to the networks. Who knows, maybe you and Cody will be watching *Logan Winston: Life of a Bull Rider* on Netflix next year."

She seemed to be taking that all in—and thinking. "All that is amazing. Your life sure is different than ours."

"It's just all part of being a champion bull rider. But the bull riding is the core. *That's* what matters to me. Staying on the bull."

She tilted her head. "I'm really glad you said that. You have a good attitude, Logan. You seem to know what's really important."

A dry chuckle came out of him. "I don't think anyone in Bear Ridge has ever said that to me."

"Eight years is a long time. You're not the same person you were."

"When I'm here, I feel like I am, though," he said, and realized how true it was, how that was what kept him off-balance as he'd drive through town, especially past places he used to frequent.

"Really? Even after all this time? Even with how much your life has changed? Your accomplishments?"

He didn't want to talk about this. Because if he did, it would dredge up the worst of his memories and he wasn't going there. "I'd better get going," he said, trying for whatever smile he could muster. He looked at Annabel, trying to focus on her, on how she'd made him feel last night and when he'd woken up just now, but he couldn't seem to get back there.

He slid out of bed and grabbed his clothes, strewn all over the place. His black boxer briefs were on top of the lamp on his bedside table. He grabbed them and put them on.

She was watching him. But she didn't look like she was enjoying the reverse striptease. In fact, she looked…a little sad. At least she couldn't hear his thoughts. She thought he was leaving so he wouldn't be here when Cody woke up, and she wanted to leave it like that.

"Hey, what's wrong?" he asked, sitting down on the edge of the bed.

"The last time you left it was for eight years," she said, and bolted upright. "Oh God, did I just say that? Forget I said that."

He wanted to run now, too. Far, far away from where his memories had taken him. But that wasn't an option. Not when he had a son.

"No matter what, Annabel, you know Cody is important to me. I won't disappear on him. I'll *be there* for him always. That's a promise."

Be the father you wished you had…

"I'll hold you to that, Logan Winston," she said, her expression softening.

You hear me? he silently said heavenward, his gaze out the window at the night sky slightly illuminated by so many stars and an almost perfect crescent moon. *I'm making a promise and I intend to keep it.*

"Last night was amazing," he said, taking her hand and kissing it. "And then some." He hoped she didn't regret it. That she wasn't going to say, *We shouldn't have and we can't again.* He was aware that he seemed to need her. Again: complicated. With a child between them, *should* they try to be a couple again, or was that asking for trouble?

Romance didn't work out for him. Never had.

The smile came back. "It was," she said.

He was hit with relief. *Good*, he thought. *Because there's no way I can be near you and not touch you.* Yeah, things were complicated. But their attraction wasn't. If it turned out that they needed to step away from this, they'd talk about it. That was the key— being honest.

"Maybe the three of us can have breakfast together," he said. "Have a nice lazy Sunday. I don't think I can handle another day like yesterday."

"I know just what you mean," she said. "Saturdays with Cody usually wear me out. Come back for pancakes at eight and then we can go to the petting zoo and we'll take our lazy Sunday from there."

He nodded, then grabbed the rest of his clothes and got dressed. He could stay in bed with her all day. A *half*-lazy Sunday.

"See you in five hours," he said, barely able to drag his gaze off her.

"See you," she whispered, tucking a swath of her long, silky blond hair behind her ear.

He tiptoed down the stairs and out the door, hurrying along the tree line to his cabin. Once inside, he went straight to his bedroom, stripped out of his clothes except for his boxer briefs, and got into bed and closed his eyes.

Not that he was planning to fall asleep just yet.

He wanted to relive every minute of what they'd just experienced. Then he wouldn't be able to think about just days from now. What it would be like to leave again—leave his child behind again, but this time *know* about it.

Leave Annabel again.

He could feel his eyelids growing heavy, and he yawned, exhausted and spent, and the next thing he knew, the sun was shining through the gaps in the vertical blinds on his bedroom windows.

He grabbed his phone to check the time. Barely 7:00 a.m. Perfect.

A long, hot shower. A mug of the great coffee his kitchen was supplied with. And he'd be ready for those pancakes and another day with Cody— and Annabel.

As he took a shower, appreciating the VIP luxury amenities and the incredible water pressure, he figured he'd again go over every second of his night with Annabel, kissing her, exploring her body, making love…but he kept hearing her voice—and not the breathy moans.

He may ask for things you can't give him. Or won't feel comfortable doing.

Like what?

Like what's going to happen in a week and a day from now. I'm just afraid to think of him getting hurt. Disappointed. Right now he's a novelty and—

Had he made a mistake by promising to make seven birthday wishes come true to make up for not being there? What if he couldn't even make the first thing on the list happen?

He was here to build a relationship with Cody. One that would be strong enough when he left to withstand the times apart. There would be lots of time apart, yes. But every time he came back, whether for a day or a few days, they'd continue to build, to cement their bond.

The last time you left you didn't come back for eight years…

That wouldn't happen again. Not now. Not when he had a child.

He had no idea what the future held. He just knew he wanted to know his son. And he was drawn all over again to Annabel.

But he'd left her once, hard as it was.

What if he *did* do the same to Cody?

Bull riding had been his priority, his reason for everything all these years.

Suddenly he lost his appetite for the pancakes.

He got dressed in jeans and a navy Henley and his cowboy boots, slinging on his favorite belt with the silver bull he'd bought after he won his first state championship. *You'll make it work*, he told himself. *You're not the same guy you were eight years ago, your insides raw and twisted, your father's words echoing in your head.*

Be the father you wished you had, he repeated to himself. Then he grabbed his wallet and keys. Time for pancakes.

And two people who were coming to mean a lot to him.

"I have my seven birthday wishes written out, Mommy!" Cody said as he came bounding down the stairs in his pj's, his mop of hair flying.

Annabel was in the kitchen, stirring the pancake batter. "Wow, will you read them to me?"

He sat down at the table, his list in front of him, a few cross-outs, lots of erasing of letters.

"Cody, honey, before you do, there's something I want to make sure you know," she said.

"What, Mommy?"

"Logan might not be able to make every birthday wish come true."

"I know that," Cody said.

"You do?" she asked.

"Yup. I already know it might be hard for him to get me the silver bike with black stripes and a matching helmet. When we went to the general store to get the poster board and we passed the bike aisle, I didn't see any silver bikes with black stripes."

Annabel felt a wobbly smile come on. Actually, that one would probably be the easiest for him.

"Okay, ready? Number one is to spend time with my father, Logan Winston."

She turned to Cody with a smile, wondering when he'd start referring to Logan as Daddy. That he was calling him Logan and by his full name, too, told Annabel he wasn't used to the idea that he had a father yet, that it was none other than his hero, and that letting himself think of Logan as Daddy was a very big deal. Times like these, she'd be so aware of how kids' heart and minds and souls were full of questions and longings and thoughts that the people closest to them weren't privy to.

A major reason why she and Logan had to be very careful with whatever was happening between them. Cody had to come first.

For a moment, she imagined Logan coming to the door, Annabel pouring the pancake batter into the pan, and instead of smiles and hellos and a kiss on the lips or just on the cheek, they'd be sniping because of an argument or one said this wasn't working out. Cody would feel the tension in the air, hear the contempt in their voices, look from one to the other, nervous and worried.

That couldn't happen. Logan had to always come to the door with a smile and a kiss on the cheek or none at all, no discord between him and Annabel.

Which seemed to mean one thing: that she couldn't have a romantic relationship with him. Like he said, no romance of his had ever worked out. Not one of hers had either—obviously, since they were both single. She had to let the idea of a second chance go for the greater good. Yeah, maybe this one time, things would work out with the champion bull rider who mostly lived on the road.

Right. Sure. I have a bridge to sell ya.

She needed to step back and focus on Cody. And let his brand-new relationship with his father be the most important thing.

She took a deep breath, sure she was making the right decision, and added a few more blueberries to her batter.

"Number two," Cody continued, "learn about Logan Winston's relatives because they're my relatives, too!"

Annabel glanced Cody. That one would be hard on Logan. She knew he didn't like talking about his family. But maybe doing exactly that, when it was

Cody asking, would be just what Logan needed. It was clear he was still holding on to so much of his troubled past. To the point that he hadn't been back to town until now. "So far, you have really great birthday wishes," she said.

Cody beamed. "Mommy, can I have some orange juice?"

"Right on the table, waiting for you," she said.

"Oh!" he said, running over with his list. He put it down and picked up his favorite plastic cup with a cowboy on it, the lasso as the handle. He took a few sips, then put down the cup and picked up the list. "Number three is the silver bike with black stripes and a matching helmet. They make those, right?"

She was almost giddy at the regular gift request. "I'm sure there's a bike shop somewhere in Wyoming that has those exact colors," she assured him. And if not, Logan would snap his fingers and that exact bike would appear on the porch, silver-and-black bow around it.

He sat down at the table, took another sip of juice, then kept reading. "Number four is to make a best friend. But I haven't made a best friend yet besides Bucky and Chappy, so I don't know if even Logan Winston can make that one happen."

So Cody was aware that Logan wasn't made of magic. That he was human. That was good.

Annabel poured the batter into the piping-hot

griddle, aware that Logan would be here for breakfast any minute.

"Number five is to have chicken nuggets and cheese fries at dinner with Mommy and Logan Winston—oh, at a restaurant, not at home."

She turned to him and grinned. "Bear Ridge Diner or somewhere fancy?"

"It doesn't matter where, Mommy. Just that we go together. Do all restaurants have cheese fries?"

"Hmm, good question. Maybe not just the way you like them at the diner. We can go there, for sure."

He beamed again. The pancakes began bubbling on top, and Annabel started flipping them. The table had been long set. After Logan had left at 3:00 a.m., Annabel had managed to fall back asleep but she'd woken at five thirty. She'd come downstairs and set the table for breakfast, getting all her ingredients ready, hoping she had enough maple syrup for three people instead of the usual two—she was glad to see she did. Then she'd taken a shower, memories of the night before washing over her with soap and water. There would be no more of that. But at least now she wouldn't wonder what sex with Logan now would be like. She knew. And of course wanted more. But she wanted to protect Cody *much* more.

"Number six," Cody went on, "is Logan Winston comes to show-and-tell at school this week."

Annabel had no doubt Logan would find that the

easiest one of all. He was used to public appearances and talking to kids. Piece of cake for him.

"And number seven is the one I want most of all," he said, jumping up and coming over to where Annabel stood, using a spatula to put the pancakes on a platter.

The doorbell rang. It was eight and Logan was here.

"I'll get it, Mommy!" he called, and rushed to the door. "Who is it, please?" he asked.

"It's Logan," came the familiar, sexy deep voice.

Cody unlocked and opened the door, flinging himself at Logan's midsection for a hug, the list held out to the side. "You're just in time for my last birthday wish," he said. "I'll start over so you can hear them, too, and then you and Mommy can hear the last one at the same time."

Logan glanced at Annabel, who hadn't moved from the stove.

The last one. The one he wanted most of all. Annabel was a little nervous.

Maybe it was to go to the state championships, though she was sure her cousins Rex and Ford already had tickets and would take Cody.

He came in and closed the door, then followed Cody, holding his hand into the kitchen.

"Can I help with anything?" Logan asked, looking at the table, then at her.

Cody sat down, list in hand.

"Nope," she said, "everything's all set. Though you can help yourself to coffee."

He did, pouring himself a big mugful and adding cream and sugar, which had required him coming close to where she stood, sliding the sausage links to another platter. "Hmm, everything smells amazing."

He smelled amazing. He was so close she could smell the soapy freshness of him, his shampoo. A memory of last night tried to sneak its way into her head but she forced herself to focus on bringing the platter of pancakes to the table without tripping.

"I'll get the sausage platter," Logan said, popping up and bringing it over. "Is your tummy growling?" Logan asked Cody as he sat back down.

"My stomach always growls when I'm hungry," Cody said. "I'm really, really, really happy you're having breakfast with us."

"Me too," Logan said.

"Want to know why?" Cody asked, tilting his head.

Logan nodded, glancing at Annabel for a moment. "I do want to know why."

"It has to do with the very last thing on my list," Cody said as he picked up a pancake and put it on his plate. "My seventh birthday wish."

"Cody, honey, please remember to use your fork to help yourself, okay?" Had she said that because she actually cared—though his grandmother did and would have given Cody a faux very stern look to help him remember, even if he only did sometimes—or because she was afraid what number seven was?

Combination of both, she was pretty sure.

"Okay, Mommy," he said, picking up the syrup and swirling it on top of the pancake. Cody would eat exactly two pancakes and two sausage links. Logan's appetite was a mystery. They'd eaten only pizza and Chinese and bacon-and-egg sandwiches during their time together.

"I can actually read the list in backward order!" Cody said, all smiles. He used his fork to cut into his pancake and took a bite. She was ready to reprimand him to eat with his mouth closed and talk afterward, but he did chew with his mouth closed.

Anything to prolong number seven. She just had a bad feeling about this.

"Okay, I'll start with number seven on my birthday wish list and then read backward. Number seven is that Logan Winston stays here with us forever!"

Oooh boy. She'd been right.

It was bad. Worse maybe than she thought.

Because he'd said *with us*. Not *with me*. He'd made this about them as a family.

And from the look on Logan's face, that hadn't been lost on him, either.

Chapter Eleven

"I mean, in between bull rides," Cody said, happily swiping a bite of pancake in syrup.

Logan swallowed around the lump in his throat. *Stay with us forever...* The word *forever* echoed in his head. He glanced at Annabel, then forked a sausage link and took a bite, giving himself a moment to think. "I'm really happy you want to spend time with me, Cody. Because I want to spend time with you, too. Why don't you hand over the list to me so I can read numbers six through one and you can eat this delicious breakfast before it gets cold. I can keep it, right?"

Cody beamed. "Of course. It's for you."

He glanced at Annabel again, who was sipping her coffee and looking very uncomfortable.

Now he understood why she'd been worried about telling him to make him a list in the first place.

Because he should have figured something like number seven would be on the list. How could he possibly make that one come true?

He took a quick scan of the other wishes. The only problematic one was the last. It made the second one, learning about Logan's family, seem like no big thing.

He wanted to thunk his head against the table. Instead, he ate his blueberry pancakes and sausages, drank his coffee, and tried to focus on the conversation instead of the list. Number seven, specifically.

"Can we?" Cody was saying. "We could say hi to Bucky and Chappy."

Cody must have asked if they could go to the petting zoo after breakfast.

"Sure," Logan said.

"Yay, the three of us are going!" Cody said, finishing his orange juice.

He glanced at Annabel. Her slightly raised eyebrow told him she knew he'd missed the first part of what Cody had said because he was ruminating on number seven.

A half hour later, Annabel having taken the day off, the three of them were heading across the path. Annabel mentioned that the guests in all six cabins for the next five days were one family, for a reunion, and the entire group was on a tour of the woods and Clover Mountain. Since the petting zoo wasn't open to the public until ten, this meant they had the place to themselves. They stayed until just before ten, Logan getting to meet Oinky the goat and Cody's chicken buddies. The adorable animals were a great distraction from Cody's list—and the woman keeping just a slight distance from him, always on the other side of Cody or hanging back a bit.

He didn't like the distance. He didn't want her "over there" or lagging behind. He wanted her beside him. He wanted to talk to her, share his thoughts about the goats and the funny-looking alpacas in their pen. He wanted to hold her hand, smell her perfume, remember last night. He definitely didn't want to forget it, which was what she seemed to be trying to do.

But *he* was the one standing in their way. And "their" included Cody, too. He couldn't stay forever.

As they left the petting zoo, Logan whispered to Annabel that they could head to a bike shop and take care of birthday wish number three, and she said sure, so he did a quick online search and found a bike shop in the next town. When Cody learned where they were headed he got very excited and told Logan all about how his current bike was just starting to get too small for him. They started walking down the path toward the parking lot by the Welcome Hut, his phone pinged with a text. Savannah.

Checking in on my favorite cowboy. How's that wrist? How's fatherhood?

It felt good to hear from Savannah. Until he came back here, until Annabel and Cody, he only had Savannah. She was family and his only family. His chosen family, as on Cody's school project.

Now Cody was his family.

And Annabel had always felt like family, right away, too, even though he left her, even though he pushed her away. He was still pushing her away.

"Excuse me a second," he said to Annabel and Cody. "Savannah's checking in."

He stopped and texted her back that the wrist felt good, that he'd been careful with it, and that fatherhood was raising a lot of questions that he didn't have answers to.

Yeah, I'll bet, Savannah texted back. You want answers? Deal with your history. Trust me on that, champ.

He scowled and pocketed his phone. His history? His questions were about his *future*. Cody was his future. The past would only drag him down. Like it had been doing the past year in particular. But that was because he was out of sorts about his father dying— alcohol-related, of course. Everett had been by himself, drinking from a bottle of whiskey while walking on a trail up Clover Mountain, and had taken a bad fall off a ledge. A yellow Lab with a pair of married hikers started barking its head off or otherwise, no one might have found him. Logan was grateful to that dog. The owners had taken the time and trouble to check out what had Marley barking like that, and they'd called the police. Logan had gotten the owners' name and sent them a thank-you with a gift card for five hundred bucks and a big box of treats and toys from a pet company online for Marley.

Savannah thought that was proof that Logan had loved his father, that he cared, even if he didn't attend his funeral. By the time Logan had left, though, there'd been no one to invite. Eight years later, he doubted that had changed. The Bear Ridge chief of police had let Logan know that his father had spent quite a bit of time in jail over the eight years, once for over a year, and that he picked so many fights that most kept their distance from him. Odd jobs on the ranch just a mile away had kept him with enough money to eat and pay his bills. Logan had called the town when he first started making money and set up automatic payments of the property taxes on the house, which Logan's paternal great-grandfather had built. At least his father would always have somewhere to live.

"Can you teach me how to ride with no hands like Ethan in my class can do?" Cody said, shaking him from his morbid thoughts. Why was he thinking about all that?

Because of you, Savannah Walsh. Grrrr.

Or because this was what was meant by *dealing with your past.*

"If your mom says it's okay," Logan said, ruffling

Cody's hair. He noticed that while the boy's hair was light brown when his own was dark brown, it was the same texture, thick and a bit wavy. When he looked at Cody, he saw Annabel, but as he glanced at Cody as the boy chattered on about how many kids in his class could ride one-handed and no-handed and who couldn't do either, he noticed that he and Cody had the same eyes, but Cody's were hazel-green. The nose was all Annabel, straight and elegant. Annabel was tall, five-eight, five-nine, and Logan was six-two, so there was no doubt Cody would be tall, too.

You are my family, he thought, a warmth spreading in his chest.

"You'll start with *one* hand," Annabel said to Cody. "When you get really good at that and there isn't a single broken bone, then we'll talk about no hands. How's that?"

"I guess," Cody complained, but in his usual good-natured way, a grin on his face two seconds later as he ran after a butterfly.

"You okay?" Annabel whispered to Logan. "That text from Savannah seemed to affect you."

"She asks questions I don't want to answer," he said truthfully, which surprised him. Annabel had a way of getting him to be honest—with himself *and* her.

They arrived at the parking area and got in Logan's SUV for the trip to the bike shop.

Logan buckled up and started the engine. "So,

Cody, I figure number one on your list is ongoing, right? Spending time together. We've been doing that and are spending today together, too."

Cody gave a big nod, looking at Logan in the rearview mirror. "Yup. Number one is definitely happening."

"And now we're making number three happen," Logan said.

Cody was beaming in the back seat. He was chattering about how silver was now his favorite color, just like Logan's and Mommy's.

A half hour later, they'd arrived at the bike shop. The moment they walked in, there was a silver bike with black stripes—in Cody's size. The three of them couldn't believe it. Annabel kept insisting that Logan must have called ahead and snapped his fingers, but he swore he didn't—and hadn't.

"Some things are just meant to be," he said.

Cody was pedaling around the front of the shop, designed for exactly that purpose, wearing his new helmet, also silver with black stripes. Truly meant to be. Logan put the bike in the back of the SUV and they headed back to the ranch, where Annabel had her own bike and Logan said he probably shouldn't ride, given that he'd need to use his wrist on the handles, but he was a runner, six miles four times a week, and he could get in a good jog keeping up with Cody.

Not two minutes into the ride, Cody went over a

twig and the bike went sideways, landing right on top of him. Luckily, it wasn't a heavy bike.

"Cody!" a young voice called. "Are you okay!"

They all turned to see a boy Cody's age running over with his own bike, his parents behind him.

"Hi, Leo," Cody said. "Are you staying at the ranch?"

"Nah, we just came to go the petting zoo and then we decided to rent bikes. This is where you live, right? You're so lucky!"

Cody beamed.

"Hi, I'm Annabel Dawson, Cody's mom, and this is Logan Winston, Cody's dad."

Logan froze for a second at the "Cody's dad." He himself had told many people that he was the boy's father. But this was the first time someone else introduced him that way.

Cody's father.

One day, it wouldn't feel so new, so strange.

Turned out Leo Larramie was in Cody's class, and Leo asked Cody if he could come over after school sometime to see his new pet hamster, Monkey, and just like that, Cody had himself a new buddy.

Logan froze again. Wasn't that on his birthday wish list? Number five? A best friend. This was sure a good start.

The Larramie family were on their way out, so they said goodbye and set up the playdate for next week.

"Wow, I made a friend, just like on my birthday

list! You made that come true!" he said, rushing to Logan and squeezing him into a hug.

Logan smiled and hugged him back. "Well, I don't know if I had anything to do with it, but I'm very happy about it."

"If we didn't get my new bike today, we wouldn't have come out on the bike path," Cody said. "And I wouldn't have seen Leo! I mean, Leo wouldn't have seen me totally wipe out. It's all because of you!"

"The wipeout, too?" Logan asked with a smile.

"Everyone wipes out," Cody said. "Even you, right?" he said, gesturing at his black wrist brace.

Logan laughed. "Even me."

Cody jumped back on his bike and sped ahead, Annabel smiling and following, and Logan jogging to keep up.

As he ran, he tried to think of the word for how he felt right now, but he couldn't put his finger on it. He just knew the feeling was unfamiliar. A good feeling, though.

He stopped dead in his tracks when he heard Savannah Walsh's voice in his head. *You're happy, dummy.*

Huh. He was happy. That was exactly what he felt. Happiness.

Had it been that long since he'd last felt this way? He was happy he won competitions, of course. And prizes. When he got new lucrative sponsorships with major companies. But this feeling was different from *that* happy.

This was…he really didn't know. But he knew it had something to do with Cody Dawson.

And his mother.

When Annabel and Cody arrived back at the cabin, Cody got busy upstairs with his reading homework for tomorrow, and Annabel called her mom, making sure she was well out of earshot, to fill her in on the past couple of days with Logan, leaving out spending last night in bed with him, of course. But she did admit there was something brewing between them and her worries. Her mom said she should do what felt right to her.

But what felt right and what was right for Cody weren't one and the same.

Maybe they are, was her mom's response.

Now, Annabel sipped a margarita at Marianna's Mexican Café, Daisy and Maisey across the table, a big bowl of homemade tortilla chips and two kinds of salsa between them while they perused the menu.

Her mother was babysitting Cody for the next two and a half hours. Dinah had been dying to hear every detail about Cody and Logan's blossoming relationship from the boy himself, and Cody had been excited to have someone to talk nonstop to about every little detail. So her mom had suggested an impromptu girls' night out, and both Daisy and Maisey were in.

After they ordered—veggie burrito for Daisy, chicken quesadilla with rice and beans on the side for Maisey, and chicken enchiladas suizas for Annabel—Daisy leaned close and nabbed a chip, swiping it in the spicy salsa.

"So…" she said, wiggling her eyebrows. "Fill us in. More kisses, am I right?"

Annabel peered around and made sure no one was in hearing distance; their table was luckily across the aisle from the row of booths. She knew she could trust Daisy and Maisey to be discreet, even with their husbands; they'd made a woman pact about just that years ago so they could be really open and not worry about Harrison or Rex—and no one had to worry about Annabel's guy since he didn't exist—knowing intimate details. "We slept together last night," she whispered, her heart pinging just saying it. Soaring and then falling and soaring.

"Whoa!" Daisy said.

"Are you back together?" Maisey asked. "Tell us everything."

Annabel sipped her delicious, icy-cold margarita. "I don't know what we are. We were talking and then he said he'd loved me eight years ago and everything inside me melted. Then we're suddenly in bed. He left in the middle of the night so that Cody wouldn't wake up and be confused—he's the most important thing. And protecting his relationship with Logan."

"But being together can only be good for Cody," Daisy said. "You two are his parents. What a love story that would be if you got back together all these years later, your son the best man at your wedding."

"Whoa. No one's talking about marriage," Annabel said, though last night, she'd done quite a bit of fantasizing about her and Logan being husband and wife, living as a family with Cody. Logan was proof that dreams could come true if you were determined and willing to put in the work. But what was the "work" when it came to rekindling a beautiful old flame? Logan didn't want to live in Bear Ridge. His life was elsewhere—three hours away. And what a life it was—or one that suited him, anyway.

"He's at the start of a two-week recuperation," Maisey said, grabbing a tortilla chip and swiping it into the salsa verde. "He's probably already bonded with Cody, right?"

Annabel nodded. There was a strong bond. "Definitely. I mean, Cody is very easy to love, but Logan is almost a natural at fatherhood. He just stepped right in—and up. There's no awkwardness between them at all."

"Okay, flash forward one week," Maisey said. "Think about what their relationship will be like. How important they'll be to each other, how much they'll mean to each other. You think Logan is walking away so fast?"

"His son will definitely trump how he feels about Bear Ridge," Daisy said, then took a sip of her frozen margarita. "Loving Cody will have more weight than hating his hometown."

Annabel inwardly sighed with how much she wanted that to be true. "I really hope you're both right."

The waitress returned with a big round tray holding their entrées.

"Remember, Maisey and I are proof that everything you're worried about is gonna be just fine."

Daisy laughed. "So true. Remember how when Harrison first came to town, it was to secretly try to steal the Dawson Family Guest Ranch out from under me and my brothers—when I was nine months pregnant and had just gotten dumped at the altar on what should have been my wedding day? If we got past that… I mean, even my brothers love him."

Annabel shook her head with a smile. "You have a very good point."

But as she dug into her incredible enchiladas suizas, she thought about her mom's advice to do what felt right. What felt right was being very cautious when it came to Logan Winston. Not getting romantically involved. Not doing anything that could result in a bad breakup, which would only end up hurting Cody. Annabel already saw how Logan dealt with bad relationships: he cut the tie. She couldn't risk that. Even if he only cut the tie with her and not with Cody—she couldn't actually imagine him doing that—the strain and stress in the air would be awful for him. He didn't need that.

Her relationship with Logan had to be strictly a parenting partnership. Friendly and warm. No romance.

Even if just the thought had her feeling bereft and missing him terribly.

Chapter Twelve

On Tuesday afternoon, Logan waited in the lineup of cars for Cody to come out the front doors of Bear Ridge Elementary School. His heart actually soared in his chest at the sight of his son with his orange sneakers and bright blue backpack, stickers all over it.

You had me at Cody Dawson, age 7, he realized. The moment he'd seen that photo in the *Gazette* in Savannah's car, Cody with his missing front teeth, the big smile, he'd felt a connection. Deep down, he'd known Cody was Annabel's. Maybe he hadn't known Cody was *his* immediately, but he'd known the boy was *special.*

Logan and Cody would spend the afternoon together, then meet up with Annabel for dinner. *We should talk,* she'd said. *After Cody goes to bed.*

He knew what that meant.

That she *did* regret the other night.

That she was worried, as she'd been when he'd just *kissed* her.

He saw Cody looking in the queue of cars. When the boy spotted his silver SUV, his eyes lit up and he waved, then ran over, his thick, light brown hair flopping.

"Hi!" Cody said, opening the back door and hopping into the car seat. Logan waited for him to buckle up, then eased out of the lane.

"Hi, yourself. What should we do today? Any special requests?"

"I was thinking about that during lunchtime and recess," Cody said. "Can we do one of the things on my list? Because it's also a new school assignment due next Monday."

Uh-oh. Logan had already taken care of the easy one: the bike. And maybe even the best friend.

"Which number birthday wish could this be?" Logan asked.

"Number two!" Cody said. "Learning about your relatives. I have to pick a family member to write about for the assignment. Can you show me where you grew up? And tell me about your parents and grandparents? And then I'll pick who I want to write about. The essay has to be eight lines this time."

Logan tried not to frown. Or scowl.

"The house I grew up is nothing special, trust

me," Logan said. "It's a disaster, really. Run-down, falling apart."

"Really?" Cody said. "But you grew up there?"

"I did. It wasn't so nice then, either. But it's worse now." Savannah had fielded a few calls from the Bear Ridge police that they sometimes caught teenagers hanging out there and chased them off and Logan should think about beefing up the locks, which half the windows didn't have. He had Savannah take care of that, but she still got two calls during the past few months. Apparently, the teens didn't do any damage; the officer who'd called noted the place had all the same issues it had the first time the cops had gone through the house to assess for damages.

Right. The hole in the wall along the hallway that led to the kitchen? His father's fist when Logan was seventeen and first said no about handing over half his paycheck from the ranch he worked at part-time after school. He had at first, but then realized Everett hadn't bought groceries with it or paid the power bill, which was about to be turned off. He just drank and gambled it away, like he'd done to his own earnings.

He suddenly heard Savannah's voice in his head. *Whatever you need to put to rest in Bear Ridge has the reins right now. Not you. And that's very dangerous. In more ways than one...*

Oh hell. Would going to see the house, a drive-by, a park out front, help put something to rest? Maybe. Probably not. He'd just get overwhelmed. And probably pretty damned sad. And he'd think about his mother, who'd once loved the shabby starter house until she realized there never would be money to fix it up.

He supposed taking Cody over would kill *three* birds. Cody would learn about his relatives for birthday wish number two and have some context about where his paternal grandparents and where his father had grown up for the essay. And Logan could tell Savannah he'd actually gone to see the old place. That he'd put something to rest. That he had the reins now.

Not that he knew that would be the case.

"Did you have a tire swing hanging from a tree in the backyard like I do?" Cody asked.

Aww, he thought, a memory of his mother pushing him as he dangled belly-flopped through the tire in the tree out front coming to mind. "I did, actually," he said.

"Is it still there?" Cody asked.

"No. It got taken down when I was older." No need to go into that story, which of course involved his father.

The house was on the outskirts of town on a rural country road a few miles from the border of another town. It was a fifteen-minute drive from Cody's school, and Logan wished it had taken longer to get there. Where was a tractor going ten miles an hour in front of you when you'd *welcome* it?

He pulled up along the edge of the lawn. Logan had a local landscaper mow the lawn as needed only to keep it from getting overgrown, so it still looked as awful as it had when he lived there. Patchy, brown in spots. Weeds. He hadn't been able to bring himself to sell it for reasons he refused to think too deeply about. He took care of the place enough so that he'd hear from the town as little as possible. Or that Savannah would, actually. She told him everything, whether he wanted to know it or not, and he was never sure if it that was a good thing or not. Probably a little of both.

"This is where you grew up?" Cody asked, unbuckling his seat belt.

"Yup. Not the nicest house in town."

"I like the color. There's a yellow bird that's always on our bird feeder and it's almost the same."

Dammit, he liked this kid.

The house was a wreck, peeling paint, broken hinge on the front screen door. His grandparents would turn over if they could see what his father had done to the house they'd built. But Cody saw the yellow of the bird pecking away at the bird feeder.

Cody grabbed his backpack beside him and unzipped, then pulled out his notebook and a pencil. "Can I ask you questions about the house and your family?"

"Sure," Logan said.

"Did your parents own this house?"

"My grandparents built it," Logan said. "Your great-great-grandparents."

"Wait," Cody said. "Can you help me spell grandparents? G-R-E?"

Logan did, Cody taking a bit to write out the long word.

"Is great spelled G-R-A-T?" Cody asked.

Logan helped him with that, too, his heart doing all sorts of flips and flops in his chest as Cody's tongue stuck out in concentration and he wrote. Wrote and erased and wrote some more.

"Can I see the house, inside?" Cody asked.

"Sure," he said, his heart now sinking at the idea of stepping foot inside.

As they walked toward the house, Logan saw someone inside, staring at him out the window of the living room. A teenager. The kid's eyes widened and Logan expected him to run for the back door to flee, but he actually came out the front door. He was lanky with a mop of dirty-blond hair and wore a long-sleeved Toni and Tony's Pizzeria T-shirt, jeans and beat-up black Vans.

The Toni and Tony's T-shirt gave the kid some points in Logan's book.

"You're Logan Winston," the teen said. He couldn't be older than seventeen. Maybe eighteen.

"I am. Who are you?"

He didn't respond. "You gonna call the cops on me?"

"Should I?" Logan asked, aware Cody was staring from him to the teenager and back again, eyes like saucers.

"I'm not doing anything. I just hang out here sometimes because it's abandoned. I don't take anything or cause any damage. Swear it."

"Okay," Logan said.

The teen continued staring at him. He seemed shocked Logan wasn't chasing him down or pulling out his phone to call the BRPD.

"Well, you know who I am. And this is my son, Cody."

"I'm seven and a half," Cody said proudly.

"I'm eighteen. I'm graduating high school in a week and can't wait. Then I'm outta here."

Yup. Logan could see *I'm outta here* all over this kid.

"You have a name?" Logan asked.

"Michael," he said.

Logan nodded. "Well, I want to show Cody around the house. I grew up here."

"I know. Everyone knows. Why don't you tear this place down and build a mansion or something?"

"Because my grandparents built this place. With their bare hands. It means something."

"So why not fix it up?" he asked.

"Because I grew up here," Logan said honestly.

Michael stared at him with complete understanding. "Gotcha."

Logan had a feeling Michael's experiences weren't far off from his own.

"There still a lot of stuff lying around?" Logan asked.

"Yeah, crap everywhere," Michael said. He looked at Cody. "Can I say crap?"

"I'm seven, not three," Cody said.

Michael grinned.

"I'll make you a deal, Michael," Logan said. "You can hang out here when you want to if you'll do me a favor."

The teen's eyes narrowed. "What favor?"

"I need to start clearing the place out. I want you to make three piles. A trash pile of clear garbage that should be thrown away. An I-don't-know-what-category-this-is pile and a keep pile—anything you think looks important or interesting or like something I'd want to see."

"Me?" he said. "How would I know what's what? I mean, I'd know a candy bar wrapper is garbage but how would I know what you'd want to see?"

"Use your best judgment. We have a deal?"

Cody stared up at Logan, and he glanced at him with an assuring smile, then looked back at Michael.

"You can start tomorrow after school," Logan added. "Take a week, no more. And then I'll be figuring out what to do with this place."

Michael shrugged. "Okay. Deal."

He came down the creaky, peeling porch steps.

"You gonna win the championships in Cheyenne?" he asked, eyeing the brace on Logan's wrist.

"I'll try my best," Logan said.

"Trying our best is all we can promise," Cody said with a firm nod.

The teen eyed him, then Logan. "Well, I guess I'll be back tomorrow. This sure was weird."

"Weird but mutually beneficial," Logan said.

The teen nodded and jogged off.

"That was weird," Cody said. "*Really* weird. Why didn't you get him in trouble for being in your house?"

"Something about him reminded him of me when I was that age. Needing a place to hang out. I didn't get along with my dad so I didn't like being home." *Here*, he thought, looking up at the faded yellow house.

"Then that was a nice deal you made him," Cody said.

"Let's head in."

Cody looked all excited, holding his notebook and pencil to his chest as they climbed the porch steps and walked inside.

There wasn't much to look at. Four rooms downstairs—living room, kitchen, a den and a bathroom. And three bedrooms upstairs. Master. Kid room. And a guest room that no one had ever stayed in when Logan was growing up. A few days after he'd gotten the news that his father had died, he'd had Savannah's assistant hire a cleaning service to clear out the fridge and cabinets of food and to wash the dishes and give the place a basic cleaning. So the house was dusty and run-down, but that was the worst of it.

"I like this house," Cody said. "Because my great-grandparents built it. And because you grew up here."

Logan knelt down in front of Cody. "I'm glad you do. I wasn't sure what to do with it but if you like it, I'll keep it. It'll be yours someday."

"Mine, really?" Cody asked, looking around in wonder.

"Yup. Just like my dad inherited it from his parents. You'll inherit it from me."

"Wow," Cody said. "Would I live in it?"

"Well, I don't know. If you wanted to, I suppose."

"You know that I think you should do it with?" Cody said. "Make a rodeo school here. The house can be where the classrooms are and there can be a cafeteria for lunch. And outside you can make a bull-riding rodeo."

Logan almost gasped. "You know, Cody, that's a really nice idea. I hadn't thought of doing anything like that." A rodeo school. Huh. He could fund it, keep it small, maybe operate it through Bear Ridge Community Services with nominal fees. Teens like he'd been, like Michael was, could learn everything from bronc riding to how to be a ranch hand to barrel racing to bull riding. His grandparents had been rodeo fans and he'd bet they'd like the idea. "Let's go out the back and look around, see if there's room," he added.

Cody beamed. They went through the living room to the sliding glass doors that led to the backyard. The place had ten acres of land. He could build an arena back here. Didn't have to be huge.

"You'll have to have rodeo clowns, too," Cody said as they stood on the back porch and stared out at the endless land.

Logan laughed. "Definitely." He used to think of this as just country, but suddenly he saw possibilities. To the point that he could hear the snort of a bull.

"You really like my idea?" Cody asked.

"I love it," Logan said. "It's a great idea. And I'm really going to think about making it a reality."

"Wow," Cody said. "Awesome!"

Logan knew his mother would like the idea, too.

I'm glad your mother is dead. She wouldn't see what a disappointment you are...

The words slammed into his head, almost taking his breath. He was aware of Cody beside him, staring out at the land, at the potential, seeing what Logan himself saw.

Don't go there, Logan thought, trying to keep his mind on Cody. On the ideas. But no. He was in his family house. He'd been thinking his mother would like the idea of a rodeo school on this property.

I'm glad your mother is dead...

That was the last thing his father had ever said to him. On the phone when he'd been at the B and B with Annabel, when he'd called to harass Logan some more because the night before hadn't been enough. Asking for money because he drank and gambled his away. Accusing.

Logan had been so shocked that he'd been struck speechless. He'd hung up on his father and that was it. They'd never spoken again.

He *had* been a disappointment back then. Yeah, he knew his father was talking specifically about not funding Everett Winston's drinking and gambling problem when he ran out of money or got fired from whatever job he'd managed to get. But his mother would have been brokenhearted to see him traveling down the road his father had taken, getting into fights at bars, drinking too much, acting like an idiot. He'd always gotten to work at the ranch on time, was always respectful and polite to his bosses, but there'd been fights with other cowboys, and once he got fired for it from a good job he had with room and board. He'd made girls who'd liked him, maybe even loved him, cry just like his father had made his mother cry.

But once he stayed on the back of that first bull, all that had gone out of his head. In those eight seconds, he'd proved to himself—and his father—that he was *something*. And every time he didn't get thrown, every win, every championship title, the medal would push his father's words further and further down until he couldn't even hear the man's voice anymore.

That was why he stayed away from Bear Ridge.

Why he hated being here.

Because he heard that voice again.

And now that word—*disappointment*—was back, applicable to being a father to a seven-year-old boy who thought the world of him before Logan had even met him, before he'd even known Cody was his.

You can change all that, Logan knew. *You're here, aren't you? In Bear Ridge. On the back porch of this house.*

Be the father you wished you had. He could hear CJ's voice in his head and he tried to make it push away Everett Winston's.

The father he wished he'd had would not get all lost in the past and let it steal his present. Steal this moment. He was standing here with his son.

His child. This precious boy.

Focus on Cody.

"What was your dad like?" Cody asked, opening his notebook up on the porch railing to a fresh page.

"Well, he was grumpy. But you want to know something? My mother was like sunshine. And she loved him. Grumpiness and all."

"Like Grammy and Grampie's cat Pringle," Cody said. "He was a real meanie. Like if you tried to pet him, he'd scratch you. They had to put him in their bedroom when I came over to visit. But they loved that cat and said he just couldn't help being mean."

Logan put his arm around Cody. "Why did they think he couldn't help it?" The question came out before he could catch himself. He shouldn't have asked something like that of a seven-year-old. The ups and downs of learning to be a dad, he knew. Luckily there were mostly ups where Cody was concerned.

"My grandpa said it was because he thought he had to be mean to people before they could be mean to him. I sort of get it. Kinda like bullies at school."

"Yeah, that's what I think, too," Logan said, his heart constricting. His dad's life had not turned out the way he wanted and he turned mean; that was how his mother had put it.

And then he when he lost her, that was it for him. He was left with a ten-year-old son he was too scared to love.

Logan froze. Suddenly his father made sense to him. He didn't forgive him, but he finally understood the missing piece.

I will spend the rest of my life making sure you feel wanted, Logan silently told Cody. *Because you are.*

Cody sat down on the porch steps with his notebook and pencil and started writing down a few words. "I think I know who I'm gonna write about for the assignment," he said. "But I haven't decided."

Logan rested a hand on his shoulder as he sat down beside him. He could sit here forever.

Which was unthinkable. Or unthinkable a few days ago. Sit here on the back steps of his childhood home? In Bear Ridge?

What the hell had happened to him? He shook his head in wonder as a warm breeze blew his hair off his neck.

"Do you think we can go out for chicken nuggets and cheese fries at the diner this week?" Cody asked.

"Definitely," Logan said. "I'll talk to your mom about it."

Cody grinned and shut his notebook.

He could imagine Annabel telling him that yes, they could go out to dinner for birthday wish number four on Cody's list. But that it wouldn't be like a date, that they had to be strictly platonic from now on. But he didn't want to be platonic. He wanted more of the other night.

You're the one whose life is somewhere else, he reminded himself. Annabel is just protecting herself and Cody.

But there was one path to follow here—and it involved leaving in less than a week for Cheyenne, defending his title, and then spending a week having the *Times* follow him around. A week in the life of a rodeo champ.

It occurred to him that the week wouldn't involve Cody. His son. But how could it not? His son was a big part of his life now. Cody would be done with school by then; maybe he could come spend the week with Logan and be part of the entire *Times* article and video.

He could spend the summer. Yeah, Annabel wouldn't like that. Her seven-year-old three hours away?

Cody could come for a week or two. Then Logan could visit for a week or two. They could make it work that way all summer long.

But something in that didn't feel like the answer. He just didn't know what it was.

Chapter Thirteen

Since Logan had picked up Cody from school and was spending a couple hours with him, Annabel had offered to work till five. She was assigned the three-thirty tour of the woods and river with the Hamiltons and the Londons, two branches of the same family, at the guest ranch for a family reunion. Unfortunately, a Hamilton and a London were getting divorced but had agreed to come to the reunion for the sake of the Hamilton and London grandmothers, who shared a birthday, which was yesterday, and both had turned eighty. Apparently, the separated couple were also trying to be civil for the sake of their eight-year-old daughter, who was already very upset that her parents were splitting up.

And to stay civil, a great-aunt had the idea to keep

them on either side of their daughter, so they couldn't argue or snipe or make passive-aggressive remarks.

They did anyway.

For the past half hour, the girl had moved far back with her cousins and was listening to Annabel's fellow tour guide give a talk on woodland creatures. A porcupine, and there were many of those in these woods, had brazenly ambled near the path, and the cousins were full of questions about them and their quills.

Meanwhile, Annabel was up front with the sniping soon-to-be-divorced couple. And getting more miserable herself by the moment.

"What happened to putting Serafina first, huh?" the husband was saying, teeth gritted, eyes narrowed.

"Oh, like you put her first? My therapist said I should start putting myself first, so this is how it's gonna be, bub. No more falling for your manipulative twisting lies by using Serafina to get me to do what you want. I'm onto you!"

"Oh please," he muttered. "It's always been about you, you, you. My therapist said *I* should put myself first!"

"Cretin!" the wife snarled, and stomped ahead.

He marched right up to her, muttering at her back. "Oh, I'm the cretin…"

Annabel had had enough. She was five minutes early to end the tour but she'd reached her breaking point. She clapped her hands and blew her whistle.

"Everyone, it's time for our break to sit by the riverside, have some water and a snack, if you'd like, and then we'll head back to the ranch."

The wife lifted her chin and ran past the husband, beelining for their daughter. The husband started to do the same, but his twin brother linked arms with him mid-rush and pulled him aside for a little chat. Annabel glanced over at eight-year-old Serafina. She was munching from a baggie of Goldfish crackers and chatting with her cousins. Meanwhile, her mother was texting furiously on her phone.

Annabel shook her head. She didn't mean to judge. But she didn't want anything these people were saying or doing to be anything she'd say or do.

And what if Logan, who had no plans to stay in Bear Ridge, no set plan for how to be in Cody's life, didn't like when Annabel would press the issue, which she would next week? Cody would have questions about when he'd see his father, and Logan would need to give some real answers.

She frowned. Was she projecting a little of the Londons' angst on her own situation? Getting anxious before she had reason to? Maybe.

But was this where she and Logan were headed? *You said you'd put Cody first. You said this, you said that...*

Arguments and snipes and bad blood?

She didn't want that for Cody. She knew Logan didn't.

So what then?

You stay away from his lips and hands. No matter how badly you want the man to kiss you and touch you and take you to bed, you remember this tour and step out of arm's reach.

Cody did come first.

She would tell Logan that they had to be platonic. She would ask him to think about his schedule as it concerned his son. She would keep things light and breezy.

But she felt anything but light and breezy right now.

She wanted all her answers this minute. Logan's intentions, his plans, his schedule.

What the hell was wrong with her? Why was she so out of sorts?

Because this isn't about Cody right now and you're beginning to realize that. It's about you and how you feel about Logan. What you want. And what you know you can't have.

Annabel bit her lip and sighed and sat down on a flat rock, trying to listen to the question a Hamilton was asking about the shortest way up Clover Mountain.

Clover Mountain. Where Cody had been conceived in a sweet little cave, a soft blanket underneath her and Logan.

She was falling in love with Logan Winston all over again.

And scared he was going to walk away from her all over again.

She sighed again. At least she was acknowledging the truth. Yes, she was rightfully concerned about Cody.

But she was very worried for her own heart.

"I saw where Logan grew up, Mommy!" Cody said when Logan brought him back to Annabel's cabin. "I went inside and everything. And Logan might even start a rodeo school there and it was my idea." Cody was chattering without a breath, his hazel eyes excited.

Logan stayed in the entryway since he wasn't planning on staying. He needed some time alone—to think or not think. To just settle his head. He could see that Annabel was surprised by all Cody had said.

"Mommy, did you ever go to the house Logan grew up in?" Cody asked as he sat on the bench by the door and untied his sneakers.

Annabel's cheeks flushed, and he tilted his head. He'd never taken her to his house during their three days together. He hadn't even lived there then; he'd had room and board with his job at the Sattler Ranch. But something told him she had gone there—maybe drove by to see it or something.

"Once, actually," she said. "I didn't go inside like you did, though. I just drove up to the edge of the front yard and stayed in my car." She glanced at

Logan, then shoved her hands in the pockets of her jeans.

"But why didn't you knock on the door to see if he was home?" Cody asked, dropping his sneakers in the basket next to the bench.

"This was after he left Bear Ridge," she said. "So I knew he wasn't there. I just wanted to see the house he grew up in for myself."

"It's yellow, Mommy. Like the bird who likes our bird feeder." Annabel had something of an awkward smile on her face. It was time to save her from this line of questions.

"You had a great idea about the rodeo school," Logan said, kneeling down and opening his arms. Cody ran into them for a hug. "I'd have to really think hard about it but I like the idea a lot."

Cody beamed. "Mommy, when do we do number six on my birthday list—go to the diner for chicken nuggets and cheese fries? The three of us?"

"Hmm," she said. "Let me check our schedules and I'll, uh, text Logan about that."

"K. Do you really have to go?" Cody asked him, wrapping his arms around his hips and looking up at him.

"Yup," Logan said. "But I'll see you very soon, promise."

Cody beamed. "Okay! I'm going up to my room."

When Cody's feet could be heard pounding on the hallway upstairs, Logan opened the door. "Well, you text me about that chicken nuggets dinner," he said. Also awkwardly.

"I will," she said. Tightly.

He wanted to bring his hand to her cheek and tell her things shouldn't be this way between them. Strained. But she was trying to put some distance between them and so was he, and he figured this was just part of that awkward stage. Tomorrow they'd go back to being friendly toward each other. And he could get back to feeling more like himself.

The problem there was that *that* Logan Winston was gone forever. His life had changed irrevocably.

He stepped outside. "Talk to you soon," he said, and then hurried down the stairs toward the path to his own cabin.

"How was seeing your childhood home?" she asked, coming out to the porch. Not letting him go that fast.

"Harrowing at first. But once Cody mentioned starting a rodeo school there, the possibilities took over the bad memories. He really has a great idea there."

Another tight smile. "You'd hire people to run it, I assume."

"I'd have to. I couldn't be there on a daily basis, of course. I'm thinking a nonprofit. Keep the fees nominal, make it accessible to people like I used to be who wouldn't have been able to afford much.

From kids to adults. But we'll see. It's just a thought right now. Something nice to do with the property."

"It's good you went," she said. "Sounds like a lot of good came out of it."

Huh. He hadn't really thought of it that way, but she was right. His head was about to explode. He stood on one side of the porch steps and she on the other side. He was aware he couldn't seem to take his eyes off her, caught as he was in her driftwood brown eyes, tall, curvy body in the pale pink tank top and jeans, and blond hair gleaming in the bright June sunshine.

I'm going to have to leave you all over again, he thought, his chest tightening. But this time, it certainly wouldn't be eight years. He'd be back every few weeks to see Cody. And he'd stay a while, as long as he could. If he had a rodeo school here, he could build himself a private practice arena at the far end of the property. That way he'd be able to stay longer stretches with Cody. He could spend time with his son and get in his practice for competitions.

"Talk to you soon," he said, again, he realized.

She gave him the tight smile and held up a hand in a goodbye, and he almost ran to her and wrapped his arms around her and told her they could figure this out, somehow make it work so that they could be together without all the trepidation and questions. But he didn't know how to do that. He nodded and headed down the steps, taking a slow jog back along the path to his cabin.

Halfway there, a text pinged on his phone. CJ Clark.

Hey, how's fatherhood going?

Logan smiled. I've been taking your advice, so it's been good.

I know this is last-minute, but if you're free, I'm making spaghetti and meatballs and garlic bread—the twins' favorite. MY favorite. 6:30 if you can make it.

Hmm. Logan did have to get out of his head. And dinner with someone else's family? That would do it. I'm in.

CJ texted him the address, and Logan pocketed his phone, already feeling better. He didn't doubt that being in the thick of the Clark family, twins, no less, would remind him in living color that this wasn't the life for him, that he wasn't a family guy, that he was a champion bull rider who lived on the road and that was his present and future. There were all kinds of families out there due to all kinds of circumstances, and Logan's would be one of them. Not necessarily traditional, but he'd make the joint custody work.

Which made him realize he and Annabel hadn't talked about that word. Words. *Joint custody*. He'd like officially to petition for that, make that legal, make sure he was listed as Cody's father; he wasn't sure if his name was on the birth certificate, and if it wasn't, maybe they could amend that. He'd consult a lawyer and get the facts.

At six thirty he pulled into CJ's driveway. He liked the house. It was a farmhouse, white, on a good three acres of land, not too far from the center of town. There was a tire swing in the front yard.

The Clark twins came rushing out to greet him. And within minutes, Logan was seated at the table in their dining room, CJ saying grace, which he didn't expect but thought was nice, the boys with their heads bowed but sneaking peeks at Logan, as he realized he was doing to them.

"I knew you could cook, CJ, but wow, this might be the best spaghetti and meatballs I've ever had." He wasn't exaggerating.

"I cooked for my brothers growing up, so I got a lot of practice. You think I'm good, you should try Jayla's chicken Parm, the twins' second favorite."

Jayla, a pretty redhead with dark brown eyes, smiled at him. "You're welcome for dinner any time. How's the Dawson Family Ranch cafeteria?"

"I actually haven't eaten there once," he said. "Cody's mom has a cabin on the ranch property since she works there, so we've eaten there or gotten food out."

"That's so nice that you're spending time together as a family," Jayla said.

Logan smiled, awkwardly, he was sure. Thing was,

being at this table felt strange. The conversations, the corrections of the twins' manners, the vote on which animated movie to watch after dinner. *Cloudy with a Chance of Meatballs* for the twentieth time or the first *Ice Age* for the thirtieth?

It all seemed so…unfamiliar. Not that CJ's upbringing had been so different from Logan's own, but he was so natural as a husband and father.

He had a child, so he *was* a family guy now, but was this the life he could see for himself? Sitting at the dinner table every night, talking about school and extracurricular activities and summer plans and road trips to a national park?

Like that's bad? Like that's hard? What the hell was wrong with him? It was the childhood experience he wished he'd had every night, but instead, it was mostly him and his exhausted, weary mother when she didn't have a double shift to make up for money troubles his father had caused.

It's just not what you're used to, he realized. And what's unfamiliar can feel strange and *other*.

He'd definitely talk to a lawyer and square away the custody questions. At least he'd know what his rights were there and when he was away from Cody for stretches of time, he'd always feel secure knowing there was a legal document.

Logan thought accepting CJ's invitation would take him out of his head? Something else he'd been wrong about.

One of the twins—Anders—picked up a long piece of spaghetti with his fingers and dangled it over his open mouth, letting it drop.

"Anders Clark, we have company! Special company, at that."

Logan smiled. "I need to see kids acting like kids, so this is good."

The twins got into a couple of small arguments, Austin Clark accidentally dipped his elbow right in his spaghetti and meatballs while reaching for the basket of garlic of bread on the other side of his brother's plate, and twice CJ or his wife had to admonish a boy for something. There was also a lot of laughter and clear love among the crew, including the brothers, despite their trying to one-up each other. *This is life as it should be*, Logan thought. *The way my childhood should have been but wasn't.*

Well, here's your chance to give Cody that childhood, he realized. Traditional family life.

A chill ran up his spine, though, and an icy prickling feeling was clawing at his chest. He couldn't figure out what that was about. Why *wouldn't* he want this? He adored Cody and he was so attracted to Annabel, and drawn to her in ways that had nothing to do with lust. So why was he looking forward to his recuperation period being over so he could get in his two days of practice back home in Blue Smoke before the competition in Cheyenne?

You're a little boy's father, he thought, feeling so

unsettled that he couldn't eat another bite. That has to come first.

But he was counting down the seconds till he got to see Cody again—and counting down the days till he got to leave Bear Ridge.

Nothing was making sense.

He blamed Savannah. Didn't she say being here would make everything okay? He'd deal with his past and then he'd stop being distracted, even slightly? Did he want Bulliminator to best him again in practice in a few days?

Maybe, he thought very tentatively.

That had him sitting up straight. What the *heck*? *Because then you'd* have *to stay.*

Chapter Fourteen

The next morning, while Logan was taking a walk along the river, aviator sunglasses and non-trademark hat pulled down low since he was in no mood to be recognized, his phone pinged with a text.

Annabel. He was aware how happy that made him.

Tonight for that chicken nuggets and cheese fries dinner at the diner? Cody asked five times yesterday and three times this morning. Upside-down smiley face emoticon.

He texted back immediately. Sounds good, then added the smiley face in the cowboy hat.

She texted back a thumbs-up.

He could keep this going all day—the connection. Why was he being pulled in two different directions? *Toward* the Dawson duo. Then in the next breath, away from them.

"Hey, Logan," a male voice said.

So much for being incognito. He looked up, relieved to see it was Rex Dawson, one of Annabel's cousins who owned the Dawson Family Guest Ranch. He'd run into Rex on the river a few days ago when he'd been with his toddler daughter. Rex was a police officer with the BRPD.

"I'm actually glad I ran into you," Logan said, taking off his sunglasses. "I wanted to let an officer know that I made a deal with a teen I found hanging out in my father's house yesterday. Michael—" He searched his brain for a last name but he realized he never got it. "Michael something. He's going to do some sorting of the stuff still there in exchange for getting to hang out there when he needs to."

Rex nodded. "That was nice of you. I know the Michael you mean. Blond, right? Round black glasses?"

"That's him."

"He's been found in there a few times and asked to leave and threatened with trespassing," Rex said. "Neighbor down the road would be driving past and see a flashlight shining and call it in. Michael's a good kid, though. Doesn't have the easiest home life."

"Yeah, I figured it was something like that," Logan said.

"You making plans for the house?" Rex asked.

"I'm actually thinking about something. Maybe a

rodeo school, nonprofit. Just in the thinking stages at this point, though."

Rex's eyes lit up. "That would be amazing. Bear Ridge loses a lot of its young people to Brewer and the bigger towns with more to offer. A rodeo school would be a great addition."

"It was Cody's idea," Logan said. "Seven years old and a genius."

Rex laughed. "I love that kid. Absolute gem."

"Yeah, he sure is," Logan said. "I wanted to thank you and Ford for carrying on Cody's grandfather's tradition of taking him to my events. That means the world to him."

"We love taking him. Man, does he get excited. Nothing like a kid to make you really appreciate life," he added. "Oh—Maisey and I would love to have you, Cody and Annabel over for dinner or a weekend barbecue," he said. "I'll talk to Annabel about it."

"Sounds good," he said.

He watched Rex continue down the path. For a man who was leaving town in a few days, Logan sure was making connections. First CJ, now Rex was inviting him over dinner.

He turned and headed toward the parking area, waved at a bunch of people along the way, and got into the SUV. It was barely 11:00 a.m., but he figured he'd see if Michael was there, if he'd started sorting the piles. The sooner he got the place cleared out, dealt with, the sooner he could really think about the rodeo school. He made a stop at the general store for trash bags, masking tape and a marker so he could make labels: Garbage. Keep. Donate. And a fourth bag and label: Don't Know.

There was a bike leaned against the house, so the kid was here. Good.

Logan walked up the porch steps, took a bracing breath and opened the door. "Hello?" he called out.

"Master bedroom," Michael called down.

Logan peered into the living room as he headed toward the stairs. There were already piles. A stack of photos, not in frames, were on the ratty couch. One candleholder beside them.

Similar in the kitchen. On the table was a small pile of kitchen stuff, basically one of everything. His dad had probably sold everything else, even if he only got fifty cents at a yard sale or something like that. Logan opened the cabinets, upper and lower. All empty. Fridge was already empty, as expected.

He went up the stairs unusually slowly, not really wanting to step foot in the master bedroom. He passed his own bedroom, which he hadn't lived in since he'd turned eighteen and left and moved to the Sattler Ranch. He'd taken what he'd wanted back then, and then when he'd left Bear Ridge for good—supposedly—eight years ago, he'd stopped at the dumpsters behind the diner and tossed it all in there. He certainly hadn't wanted his yearbook.

Though if he had it, he could look up Annabel; she would have been a freshman.

He stopped at the master bedroom his parents had shared, then where his father had slept when he wasn't passed out on the couch or the porch. Michael was sitting on the floor, going through a big wooden box, a hope chest he was pretty sure they were called.

"This is all for the Keep pile," Michael said.

Logan peered over his head. The chest was maybe a quarter full. "Yeah? Not even an 'I don't know'?"

"Nah, it's all keepsake stuff," Michael said, glancing back for a moment over his shoulder at Logan. "You know, the stuff moms like. Some old really bad drawings by Logan Winston, age six. Age seven. Here's one where you must have been like two." He chuckled at his own diss. "Bunch of diaries from like twenty years ago. Ten of them."

Ugh. Had his mother kept diaries? Ten? For every year he was born until she died, maybe. Logan's heart squeezed.

"And some letters that look old, too." He pulled the lid closed and stood up. "There's a pile on the bed, that's all donate stuff. Your parents' old clothes and shoes. A couple of suitcases. There wasn't much in the whole house."

"Yeah, I noticed. My father must have sold stuff over the years."

"So you're gonna sell this place?" Michael asked.

Logan looked around the room, at the six-drawer

cherry dresser and matching bed, both of which had seen better days. The rug that had always been there for as long as he could remember, geometric pale blues and creams. "I haven't yet, so I don't think so." He could have done that anytime over the past year. Hired a company to clear and clean it out and sold it as is. He would have donated what he got for it to a charity his mother would have supported. "I'm thinking about starting a rodeo school here. Low cost. For people like I was when I lived here—no money but big interest in rodeo."

Michael's eyes widened. "Really? Like me, too."

"Yeah? You're interested in competing?"

"Nah. Not that part. I want to work behind the scenes. Doing what, exactly, I don't know."

"There's a lot behind the scenes. Tell you what. If you do your own research and learn about rodeo in general and get more of a sense of what interests you, I'll get you an entry-level job at the Blue Smoke rodeo, if you're interested."

Now Michael's eyes were like saucers. "Why would you do that?"

"Takes one person to give you a break when you need one. I had that person. And now I'm paying it forward. Besides, you did a good job here."

"You'll really get me a job at the rodeo in Blue Smoke?" Michael asked. "I'm dying to get out of this town."

"Well, I'm leaving in a week to practice at the

arena for two days, then I'll be on to Cheyenne. You can drive down with us to Blue Smoke and I'll get you hooked up. There are bunkhouses there, too."

"Whoa," he said. "Is this really happening? Nothing good ever happens to me."

"I used to think that," Logan said. "But there were a lot of good times when I was growing up. Just so many bad ones that they were all I thought about."

"Yeah."

"I'm gonna go through this stuff while I'm in town," Logan said. "You're welcome to stay here if you need to."

"I do," Michael said. "I had a live-in job at a ranch as a hand but I got fired last week because someone lied about me to the boss. It was about a girl and it was a lie. He was just pissed that she liked me and not him. I didn't even know he liked her."

"I know how that goes. I was in that situation a few times. You like this girl?" Logan asked, thinking of himself holding hands with Annabel, walking through the flurries in the park, feeling like he had everything when an hour before he met her, he had nothing.

"I more than like her. Maybe once I get settled in Blue Smoke and can afford my own apartment, maybe she'll come down there."

"If she's special to you, don't let her get away," Logan said.

"She is and I won't."

Logan smiled. He could already see Michael was smarter and had it more together than he did a few years older back then.

"Since I'm done, I'm gonna go to the library and use the communal computers to do that rodeo research."

"Good plan. See you around."

Michael nodded and left, his entire demeanor different. The kid had purpose. Now that was a lot like Logan had felt when he finally decided to leave Bear Ridge all those years ago. He had a purpose and a plan and he'd done all right for himself. Better than all right. He had a feeling Michael would, too. And this time, a special girl wouldn't get left behind.

Got an hour or so? came a very unexpected text from Logan.

She typed back, Actually yes. Cody's at his playdate with his classmate and new hamster, so I'm free till I pick him up at 5:30.

I could use some help going through stuff at my dad's house. I'm here now.

Her heart squeezed. Be there in fifteen minutes.

For someone who was about to give him the "we have to be platonic from here on in," she sure was acting like this was some kind of date. She'd rushed upstairs to her bathroom and added a little mascara and lip gloss, ran a brush through her hair and left it loose, and changed into her favorite jeans and a flowy floral tank top. Then she brewed fresh coffee and put it into two thermoses, his fixed the way she knew he liked it, and filled a Tupperware container with the treats her mother had brought over earlier from the bakery.

She was in her car with the coffee and snacks, halfway to the house, when she realized she'd better be careful. She wasn't acting like a woman who knew she had to emotionally distance herself, *romantically* distance herself from the man who had her heart all over again.

Maybe given that he was Cody's father, there was no emotionally distancing. But she did have to put the kibosh on anything else.

She pulled into the gravel driveway. Though the house wasn't in great shape, it looked no worse than it had that one time she'd stopped in front to see it eight years ago. Just run-down. The yard was mowed and the trees out front were beautiful. The house was on a rural country road ten miles from the center of town and you couldn't see neighbors on either side. The acreage was clearly behind the house, where the arenas and stables and pens would be built, if Logan went ahead with his idea for a rodeo school.

It really was a great idea.

He must have heard her car because he opened the door before she even got to the porch.

Had she not been carrying the bag with the coffee

and scones, she might have thrown her arms around him and hugged him tight. She could see the tension on his face. Being here wasn't easy for him. Going through his father's things, his mother's things, too, had to be bringing up all sorts of memories. Her resolve to keep her hands to herself would have gone right down the porch steps with the chipmunk she just saw scurry by. The urge to comfort him, to be there for him, was just so strong.

Add to that the intense physical attraction and…

"I brought sustenance," she said to get herself back on track. "Coffee and treats from the bakery that my mom brought over this morning."

"I need both," he said. "Definitely the coffee."

She handed him the thermos with the coffee the way he liked it. A little cream, a little sugar.

"Thank you for this," he said. "And for coming. I've been here for hours, actually. The eighteen-year-old I caught in the house, the one I made the deal with to sort through the piles, he actually did a great job. And there's not even that much to go through. But I can't even bear to look closely at the 'Keep' piles. Some photographs in the living room and a hope chest upstairs. Everything else is either 'donate' or 'trash.' I've already bagged all that up."

"Anything get to you in the 'donate' pile?" she asked.

"Yeah. And they were mostly clothes and shoes that were all too familiar. My father's favorite belt that he liked to start taking off to threaten me with. An old red-and-black Western-style shirt he used to wear a lot. It was his favorite shirt to wear out drinking with pressed dark jeans. I got chills just from seeing it, Annabel. I'm supposed to look at photos and keepsake stuff?"

"Well, maybe you shouldn't look. I can just bag it up and mark it 'Keep.' No one says you have to rush this. You can save it for another time."

"But when?" he asked. "Savannah thinks the reason I got injured in the first place is because I haven't dealt with my past or my father's death. She thinks I've been off-balance and distracted all year because of it."

"You agree?" she asked.

He nodded. "I wasn't planning on dealing with any of this, actually. I came because I wanted to see you again. To tell you I was sorry for how I left things all those years. To find out if I was way off base for doing a little math in my head and thinking Cody Dawson, age seven, of Bear Ridge, could be my child. I didn't want to delve into my family history or even think about it."

"I guess Cody took care of that," she said. "With the family tree and his birthday wish list. Needing names. Wanting info."

"So now I'm here, in my childhood home, which I vowed never to step foot in again. Dealing. And how could it possibly help? I feel like hell."

She took the thermos out of his hand and set it on the coffee table, and then walked into his arms. Resolve, be damned. This was just a comfort hug for him. Nothing more.

Except then he tipped up her chin. And kissed her. His lips were so warm.

"I vowed not to kiss you again. And definitely not to end up in bed with you again. And here I am, in your arms. Kissing you."

"Maybe making absolutes isn't the answer," he said. "Maybe we both just have to take things day by day. Like I've been doing with being back in town."

"Except I'm looking to get my heart broken again. I can't get all turned around over you, Logan Winston. I can't let my love life interfere with Cody's happiness. And if I'm all out of sorts, it'll interfere. You and I need to be rock solid. That means being platonic. Caring about each other, sure. But platonic."

He nodded slowly and took a step back, picking up the thermos and taking a long drink. "You're such a good mother."

"I just love him so much," she said.

"Platonic, then." He nodded firmly. "I won't kiss you again. I'll want to. But I won't."

"And I won't fling myself into your arms. *I'll want to.* But I won't."

There was something bittersweet in his expression, in the bit of smile he gave her.

"Are we still on for dinner?" he asked, putting down the thermos.

"Oh, we *have* to be," she said. "I thought Cody talked nonstop about meeting his friend's hamster? The chicken nuggets and cheese fries eclipsed that this morning on the way to the bus."

He smiled. "I wonder why it's so important to him. Enough to be on his birthday wish list and to talk about it so much. I mean, isn't it just the three of us going to the Bear Ridge Diner?"

Annabel tilted her head. "Huh. You know, I really didn't think about it beyond exactly that. Chicken nuggets and cheese fries are his very favorite meal. And we're…his parents."

"Yeah, you must be right. I've been reading into everything lately, I guess. Cody is pretty much face value."

She laughed. "He sure is. So should I pick up the top photo and tell you what it is? Prepare you? How do you think it'll go easier on you?"

"I think I just need you here," he said.

Her heart cracked open—again, she realized. She loved this man. She shouldn't, not in the way she did—anything but platonically—but she was in love. How she was going to watch him leave, drive off from the gates, was beyond her.

He sat down on one side of the pile of photos stacked up, and she sat on the other. "Okay. I'm picking it up," he said, closing his eyes. "I'm opening my eyes."

The photo, in a peeling thin gold frame, was of his parents years ago. They both looked no older than early twenties.

"God," he said. "Look at them. Such a beautiful couple. Everything ahead of them. What the hell went so wrong? Why did my father end up with a drinking problem?"

"Maybe he had demons he never dealt with and so drinking helped make them go away?" she said softly. "I really don't have any answers when it comes to either question."

"He had everything to be happy about," Logan said. "This beautiful wife, inside and out. She was the kindest person. Why did she love him so much when he was such a jerk?"

"He probably changed slowly and gradually," she offered. "Then one day, there's more bad than the good but she was left with all the love she's always felt. And she probably thought she could help him, help get him back to who he was when she first fell for him."

Logan put the photo down on the coffee table, turning it upside down. "He didn't deserve her."

He grabbed the next photo, not looking at it until it was right in front of his face. Then he smiled. It was Logan, seven or eight. Two front teeth missing just like Cody. "When I first saw the photo of Cody in the *Gazette*, I looked for you in his face and thought I could see a resemblance even though he's somewhere between us in coloring. But now that I look at this, I realize he looks more like me than I realized. The shape of the eyes, right? And something in the expression."

"Definitely. I've always seen that even though he does favor me."

Logan took another long sip of his coffee, then put the thermos back on the side table. "I'm surprised my dad didn't stomp on this and leave the broken glass everywhere or draw devil horns on my head."

"That's the thing about arguments. The next day, that same anger isn't there and you look at a photo of your child from twenty years ago and a rush of good memories come washing over you."

"Nice try, Annabel. But I doubt my father ever picked up a photo of me and had that experience."

"Oh, I'll bet he did."

"He told me he was glad my mother was dead, that I'd be a disappointment to her. You remember I got a call when we were at the B and B? It was him. He wanted me to drive home to give him a hundred bucks so he could drink and gamble. And I said no. And he said what he said. It was the last time we spoke."

"Oh God, Logan. I'm so sorry." She grabbed his hand and held on to it. "It's worse than I ever could have imagined. And I tried to imagine what that phone call was about. I was pretty sure it had to be your dad."

He let out a breath and leaned his head back on the couch cushion. "People always say, I didn't mean it, sorry. But he never did."

"Well, he couldn't have, Logan. You changed your number. You were unfindable for a long time. And when he could find you, you were really making a name for yourself. Maybe he felt intimidated and just stayed back."

He was staring at her. She couldn't quite tell if he agreed with anything she said or if she'd upset him. "Or maybe he meant it. Period," he said, his voice sounding far away.

Oh, Logan. She realized right then that this was what had Logan Winston so tied up in knots. One drunken line from his father that had stayed lodged inside his heart like a bullet for almost eight years.

"This was a mistake," he said, standing up abruptly, putting the photo down. "I need to get out of here. I'm sorry I got you involved in this crap, Annabel. I need to get out of here. I'm sorry." His voice was breaking.

He rushed outside and was in his SUV and halfway down the road before she could even blink.

Her heart squeezed. *You can run but the past stays with you, Logan,* she thought, going back inside. What he needed to help dislodge that bullet was in this house, she knew. And she was going to find it. She went back into the living room and looked through all the photos. She found just what she was looking for.

Then she headed upstairs to the master bedroom and the keepsake chest where she had a feeling she'd find the smoking gun.

What she wasn't so sure about was whether they were still on for chicken nuggets and cheese fries. Logan was hardly in any headspace to be present for Cody. And she knew Logan wouldn't want to be all broken up while making one of his birthday wishes come true.

She had a half hour before she was supposed to pick up Cody. An hour till they were supposed to be at the diner, the three of them.

She went into the master bedroom and opened the hope chest. She had thirty minutes, tonight anyway, to find what she needed to save Logan Winston from himself.

Chapter Fifteen

What Logan needed, he realized as he drove a little too fast back to the Dawson Family Guest Ranch, was a ride on a horse. His horse, Sand Dune, but she was three hours away. But the Dawson ranch had a stable full of beautiful horses. He'd go riding, get his head together, and then he'd take Cody and Annabel out to the diner. He was not messing that up because he'd let his past get the better of him.

He'd walked out on Annabel—again. Not quite the same scenario, but that was what it had felt like. He'd apologize, though it wouldn't make what he did any more acceptable.

You're a runner. You leave. It's what you do.

But he *couldn't* do that to Annabel. Or Cody. He had to set the guidelines with how they were going to have joint custody, get back to his life, and he'd follow the visitation schedule to a tee. No matter what happened, what was going on in his life, if his past had a stranglehold on him and it was his week to visit Cody or have Cody spend time with him, he'd be there for his son.

He'd call a lawyer in the morning and get that squared away. He was leaving in a few days. And like Annabel had said she wanted, he also wanted them to be on solid footing.

He felt better already.

Then he remembered Savannah saying he couldn't even lift a horse's rein. Dammit. He scowled at his wrist brace. He wanted to tear it off and chuck it off Clover Mountain.

But of course, though the necessary brace would be gone, the injury would remain.

He texted Annabel that if she still was speaking to him, he'd meet her and Cody at their cabin in a half hour and they'd walk over to his SUV for the drive to the diner.

I'll always speak to you, Logan. See you soon.

Relief flooded his chest. Yes. This was what she was talking about. Solid footing. One of them always had to have the other's back if one of them was acting like an idiot. That would always be him, he had no doubt.

He took a good walk behind his cabin, breathing

in the fresh almost-summer air, stopping to watch a family of porcupines, listening to the birds, particularly a persistent woodpecker. Nature was always a balm.

He headed back to his cabin, took a quick shower and got dressed, recalling how just days ago, he'd donned his tux so that he'd be dressed to the nines for the biggest occasion of his life: when his son would learn that Logan was his father. He'd never forget that moment. That talk in Cody's bedroom.

Tonight, he'd push all thoughts of his childhood home and his father from his mind. Tonight would be about Cody. About being a father first.

The way it should be.

But how did being a father and a champion bull rider both come *first*?

He froze as the question slammed into his head.

They couldn't both come first.

Chapter Sixteen

Annabel was craving the Bear Ridge Diner's black bean burger and sweet potato fries, but tonight was about chicken nuggets and cheese fries, and so that made ordering easy. Three of the same please. At least she and Logan got to choose their dipping sauce. Ranch for Logan and honey mustard for her. Cody wasn't at the sauce-liking stage yet.

Logan's presence in town still hadn't become any less a sensation, so he'd had a crowd around him when they'd first arrived, which he handled like he always did. Smile, wave, and say he was excited to try his son's favorite meal here. That got lots of *aahs* and *how sweet*, and they were finally in their booth, way in the back, Logan facing away from the dining room.

As Logan and Cody sipped their lemonades and

chatted about his new friend's hamster, Annabel's mind drifted to what she'd found in the keepsake chest in Logan's father's house. She'd only had the chance to go through about half of the stuff. She'd read four of his mother's diaries, which explained a lot, and two she'd put aside because she thought he either should read them or would enjoy them. But she was hoping for something concrete from his father that she could show Logan, something the man had saved—like proof he'd gone to Logan's rodeo events, that he even knew his son was a champion. Something, anything that would serve to negate or counter what Everett Winston had said to Logan the last time they spoke. But she hadn't found anything that would help before she'd had to leave to pick up Cody from his playdate on time.

She'd ask Logan if she could go back tomorrow and do a sorting of her own for him. Most of what she saw was indeed keepworthy but not all was *see*-worthy, not when it came to Logan's peace of mind. She had a feeling that Logan would take her up on that offer to avoid having to do it himself—or go back in the house at all. His time here was coming to an end, though, and if he was going to turn the property into a rodeo school, he'd have to clear out the house. But she could make it easier.

Three plates of chicken nuggets with sides of dipping sauce and fries covered in gooey cheese arrived. They dug in, and Annabel had to admit that Cody's favorite dinner was darn good. Logan ate up half in no time, making Cody's day.

Cody forked a gooey fry. "You've made almost all my birthday wishes come true," he said to Logan, gobbling up the fry. "We've spent time together, that was number one. And number two was learning about your relatives, and I did. I even got to see where you grew up. And number three was my new bike. And number four was a best friend and Leo and I already have plans to build a sand fort at recess tomorrow."

"That's awesome," Logan said, biting into a nugget.

"Then number five—" He scrunched up his face. "What was number five?"

Annabel smiled and sipped her lemonade. "I think it was this. Coming here for this delicious dinner."

"Or was that number six?" Logan asked. "Oh wait—I think number six was me going to show-and-tell at your school. Which I'm doing tomorrow at two thirty."

"Yay!" Cody said. "Oh wait. Not yay."

"Why not yay?" Logan asked. "You don't want me to go to your school?"

With a frown forming, Cody put down the fry he'd been about to eat. "I just remember Mommy saying that soon after show-and-tell you would have to go back to where you live so you could practice for the big competition. You won't be in the VIP cabin anymore. I won't see you every day."

Annabel's heart squeezed.

Logan reached for Cody's hand. "I won't be here every day, but I'll still call you every day."

"Really?" Cody asked, brightening some. "You will?"

"Yup. How about if I call before bed every night. So you always know to expect it. I'll get to hear about your day and say good-night."

"And I'll get to hear about your day and say good-night," Cody said, now smiling. He bit his lip. "But I just realized something. If you're leaving so soon, how will you make number seven on my birthday wish list come true? It's the one about you staying here with us forever." He looked from Logan to Annabel and back to Logan. His little face was serious. And he was waiting for an answer.

Which was plain to see that Logan didn't have. He picked up his glass of lemonade but then put it back down.

"Cody, I can't make that birthday wish come true exactly as you wrote it down. I mean, I do have to go back to Blue Smoke and practice for the championship. And then I have a newspaper following me around for a week, so I'll need to stick around there, but I was hoping you might be a part of that since the newspaper wants to learn about my life. And you're a big part of my life now. So maybe I can see you a few days during that week. I'll have to arrange that with your mom."

"Will I be able to go? Will I be done with school?" he asked.

Annabel felt Logan looking at her for help with

that one. Of course he didn't know when Cody got out of school. There was a ton he didn't know about Cody's life. His pediatrician's name. If Cody was allergic to anything, which he wasn't. There was time to learn all these kinds of things. But right now, Logan was in the fun part of parenthood, when there was a hell of a lot more to it than dinners out and bike rides.

"I'll check the dates," Annabel said fast. "We'll see, okay, honey?" She tried not to let her frown take over her face.

"But you made all the other wishes come true," Cody said to Logan. "So can't you make number seven come true, too? Don't you want to stay?"

Logan took both Cody's hands. "I do want to stay. But I do have a job, too. People are counting—"

Annabel realized he'd caught himself. He'd been about to say that people were counting on him. When he had a little boy counting on him.

"I'm going to talk to your mom about making sure I see you a lot," Logan said. "We're going to work out a schedule, okay? A real schedule."

"So I'll know when I'll see you?" Cody asked, forking a fry and brightening a bit.

Logan nodded. "Yes. You'll definitely know in advance."

Cody nodded. "Okay. I like knowing when I'm doing stuff. And I definitely want to know when I'll see you again."

Logan looked relieved.

Annabel just wanted to cry.

* * *

Logan paced around the living room of his cabin, his son's words echoing in his head, in his heart.

So you can't make number seven come true? You can't stay?

He grabbed his phone and FaceTimed Savannah.

"Hey there, Champ. How's the wrist? How's fatherhood? Gearing up for getting back to practice?"

Logan explained about the birthday wish list for the seven years he'd missed. "Maybe you can cut back my schedule from now on, Savannah. Let's keep the big competitions a priority but cut way back on promo. If I stay a champ, I'll always have press. I don't have to do as much promo as you have me doing now."

"True, but all the promo leads to even more prestigious and lucrative sponsorships and spokesperson gigs," she reminded him. "But I hear ya. And dammit, I'm proud of you."

"Proud of me? I'd thought you'd be yelling your head off."

"No way, Logan. You're a little boy's daddy. And I can see how important, how meaningful that is to you. Trust me, if you didn't ask me to cut back on your schedule, I'd tell you you should be freeing up time to spend with that cutie-pie."

"You never fail to surprise me, Savannah."

She smiled. "I keep telling you that's why you pay me the big bucks."

"Speaking of bucks, I have an eighteen-year-old

named Michael Finnegan who I want to help out. He's a good kid with a background like mine and needs a break. He wants to learn behind-the-scenes rodeo. If he rides back with us to Blue Smoke, can you take him under your wing and get him hooked up at the arena with a job that comes with room and board at my recommendation?"

"You bet, you old softy," she said. "Damn, but fatherhood has changed you."

"Nah, I'm the same," Logan said.

After they disconnected, Logan went out to the patio and dropped down on a chaise, staring up at the night sky. No stars yet.

Was he the same? He felt the same. Well, except for the major change in his life. And the big hold that a four-and-a-half-foot-tall adorable boy had on him.

Cody's sweet face flashed in his mind. And the words from birthday wish number seven echoed in his head.

Stay forever. Forever. Forever. Forever.

That numb feeling was coming over him as it always did when something was wrong, when something was bothering him—down deep.

He could barely tolerate the idea of having to go back to his father's house to gather up all the Keep piles into boxes and move them somewhere—how could he possibly stay in Bear Ridge *forever*?

He'd rent a storage unit for his father's stuff. He had a basement in his condo, but he didn't want the boxes there. Maybe he'd take a couple of the photos. The ones of him and his mom during the short ten years they were together on this earth, not that there were many.

His phone pinged with a text. Annabel.

I know that was hard. Maybe I could make things a little easier in another area by culling the Keep piles at your father's house. I could stop by tomorrow between my tour and when you and Cody return from school.

I'd appreciate it, he wrote back. He had no doubt she'd know what he'd actually want to see and what could be tossed. Thank you, he added.

Of course, she wrote back.

Of course *for her*. Because she was a good, kind, thoughtful person and he was lucky to have her in his life.

She was a great mom. And they'd always be connected because of Cody. That also helped him feel better about having to leave very soon.

His phone pinged again. This time it was Savannah.

The Cheyenne Daily will run that interview with you with the video and photos of your medal room tomorrow, by the way. Looks great. Link attached.

Cody clicked on the link. The video showed him in the "medal room" of his condo, which was really just a walk-in closet he'd never be able to fill with clothes, but it worked perfectly for his trophies and medals and framed photos from magazine and newspaper shoots.

Over the past seven years, he'd accumulated quite an impressive number of shiny trinkets to mark his wins. He had the first ribbon he ever won—from the first time he'd stayed on the eight seconds. That was probably the one that meant the most, strangely enough. He'd been so determined, so sure he could do it, and then he did.

He'd always figured he'd enter competitions for as long as he could stay at the top and he'd know when he was ready to move on, to coach or open a school, as he was thinking seriously about. He had a few more years in him, he was pretty sure. Keeping him moving, on the road, never settling down for long. Just the way he liked.

Keeping him far away from Bear Ridge in his mind, in his thoughts.

But that was *before*. Now Bear Ridge would be bursting into his head and heart constantly. Cody. Annabel.

He wondered what that would do to him in Cheyenne. He'd been distracted in a vague, bad way this past year because of his father's death.

Now he'd be distracted in a concrete good way. So would that help him stay on the bull? Or would the thought of Cody riding his silver bike with the black stripes, matching helmet on his head, down the river path, see him thrown ten feet in the air. Would imagining Annabel Dawson naked beside him, her head on his chest, his hand stroking her hair, calm him or distract him to the point that he'd be on the arena ground in two seconds?

He'd find out in a few days.

Because he *would* be leaving. He had to go. The road, the rodeo, was where he belonged.

His heart would be staying behind, though.

The next day at noon found Annabel leading a tour in the woods. This time it was a girls' day out for the family reunion group, so only one half of the divorcing couple was part of the bunch huffing it along the slight incline they were now on along the riverbank. Her name was Davida and she was talking nonstop about her husband, how terribly mediation was going and how she wasn't going to let him keep her from getting her due.

"You should be more focused on Serafina," one of the great aunts said. "Not yourself."

"My therapist said—" Davida began, stabbing her walking stick into the ground.

"Your therapist is a moron," one of the grandmothers put in. "All you're going to do is prolong your agony and your daughter's. When you should be focused on her—her feelings. Her entire world is falling apart."

"Thanks for the pep talk, Harriet, but—" Annabel had a feeling Harriet was the husband's grandmother.

"No buts!" the other grandmother bellowed. "You listen to Harriet. That girl needs you right now. But you're forcing extra court dates so you can be certain phases of the moon and all school choir concerts and plays are *your* days with Sera? If you and that William met with the mediator next time and both of you put yourself in Sera's shoes, you'd act like caring parents. Not rabid wolves."

"Little harsh, Mom," a woman named Eloisa said, who she knew was the divorcing woman's mother. "But very true," she said gently to her daughter. "You're hurt, but it's your little girl who's going to suffer more than she has to."

"Yeah, while you get what you want," the husband's mother put in.

"Oh, right, like I want to be getting divorced. I'm not the cheater!"

"He did cheat," the maternal grandmother said.

That shut everyone up.

"I just want him to suffer," Davida said. "You get it, right, Annabel," she added, rushing up to where Annabel was in front of the group—and trying very hard not to listen to their awful conversation. She'd kept inching over to the right, hoping the river current would drown out their voices, but it was such a beautiful day and the current was too gentle for that.

Annabel tilted her head. "What do you mean?"

"Well, I mean, it's an open secret about the situation with you and Logan Winston—and your son," Davida said. "According to what I've heard, you never even told him you were pregnant but he found out because the boy's photo and name and age was in the newspaper or something, and he figured it out. So now he has a surprise son."

Annabel inwardly sighed. Everyone else had stopped talking and was clearly waiting for Annabel's response.

"But there had to be a reason you didn't tell him," Davida went on. "I mean, the man is hot and rich and single—a champion bull rider. And you had his son and never told him? He must be an awful person. Otherwise, you'd be rolling in his child support and not forced to lead tours in the buggy woods."

Annabel did not like this woman one bit. She was pretty close to hating her guts. But she would remain professional. She represented the Dawson Family Guest Ranch, and she wasn't about to let this woman—a woman led around by pain and stress—get the better of her.

"I understand that you feel a strong urge to protect yourself," Annabel said. "But your family is right. Your little girl has to come first. I put my son first and let that be my guide in this new world I found myself in. If you did put Serafina first, made that conscious choice, your entire focus would change. You'd operate out of fairness, not rage, for one."

"But I *am* pissed," Davida said. "I'm so angry." Her face crumpled and she covered her face with her hands. "How could he do this to me? We were a family," she wailed, and the women in the group, all of them, rushed around her.

"And you deserve to be," the husband's mother said. "But I agree with Annabel."

"Me, too," the husband's grandmother said, putting an arm around Davida. "You'll always be family, no matter what. We love you and we love Sera."

Davida swiped under her eyes. "I'll try harder," she said with a wobbly nod. She turned to Annabel. "Can we head back? I want the special in the cafeteria, the hot pastrami and potato salad and sour pickle."

Annabel smiled and put a hand to her shoulder. "Absolutely. Lunch!" she called out, and a cheer went up.

But as they all turned around, anticipating that lunch special, Annabel realized that in her focus to put Cody first, she expected Logan Winston to somehow stay in Bear Ridge to be a full-time father and give his son 100 percent. Was she asking him to give up his career, the spotlight, his adoring fans? That was what Cody's seventh birthday wish was all about—staying here with them. Forever.

It wasn't right to ask him to give up the life he'd built. All this time, he'd been trying to compromise, to make it work, to create schedules he'd stick to, but

Annabel had been so focused on Cody's heart and her own that she'd forgotten to think about Logan's.

She had to let him go. *She* had to compromise. Even it meant breaking her heart herself.

Chapter Seventeen

When Cody's teacher, Ms. Gattano, opened the floor to questions after his talk about bull riding to her second grade class, a boy with red hair in the front row shot his hand up with great enthusiasm.

Logan glanced at his name tag. Ethan. "Hi, Ethan, what would you like to ask?"

"Did you ever tell Cody the answer to the question that he wrote about in his essay? About what you say to the bulls when you're riding them?"

Logan smiled. "I sure did. I told him that I tell the bulls that even though they're not going to throw me, even though I'm going to hold on super tight, sorry, that they're still awesome and shouldn't feel bad."

The boy grinned. "Do they answer back?"

"They snort," Logan said, doing a very bad job of letting out a snort to illustrate.

The class laughed.

A dark-haired girl's hand shot up. Logan pointed at her with a smile.

"Mr. Winston, I heard people saying that you just found out you were Cody's dad. Is that true?"

Logan felt his cheeks get hot. Ms. Gattano stood and said, "Maggie, that's a very personal question and our Q and A is supposed to focus on bull riding, okay, honey?"

"Okay," Maggie said, frowning. Cody was looking around at his classmates and frowning, too. The question was just hanging in the air, and that wasn't good for second graders. Or recess.

"Well, I don't mind answering that question," Logan said. "It's true. I didn't know that I had a son. But when I found out, I was so happy. I love Cody with all my heart."

Tears stung the backs of his eyes as he realized how true that was. No wonder it had come tumbling out of his mouth. He *did* love Cody—his child.

He looked right at Cody, who was beaming, and some kids started to clap. Even Ms. Gattano was wiping under her eyes.

"So are you gonna stay here and be Cody's dad now that you know or go back to bull riding?" another boy asked.

The room got very quiet and still. Especially Cody, who hadn't moved a muscle.

This was why the teacher had stood up to put a stop to the personal questions. Because one would lead to others. Like this—the biggie. Logan mentally shook his head. He'd messed up.

This time, when Ms. Gattano hurried to the front of the room and announced that they were out of time and could everyone thank Logan for coming in and talking to them about bull riding, he let her.

The teacher had prearranged to let him and Cody leave a few minutes early so they wouldn't be mobbed by students and parents at pickup. He was grateful for that, too.

He thought about the appointment Savannah had made for him with a local orthopedist a couple of hours ago. The doc had examined his wrist, taken an X-ray and declared the wrist healed. Logan could practice as early as tomorrow. Which was perfect timing.

He walked down the empty hall with Cody, the boy's backpack on one shoulder. Cody slipped his hand into his. Logan's heart squeezed in his chest again at the little hand clutching his.

"You okay?" Logan asked.

Cody nodded. "I know you're coming back." The boy looked up at Logan and smiled, and Logan's heart was lost to him. He didn't even know such a feeling, a sensation, existed until that moment.

"That's a promise," Logan said. "I'll always come back. I love you, Cody."

Cody's smile lit up his whole face. "I love you, too, Daddy."

Logan gasped inwardly. That was the first time Cody had called him Daddy; the boy had pretty much avoided calling him anything.

He thought his heart was lost a moment ago? He didn't know the half of it.

Annabel had sorted through the photos left on Logan's dad's couch. She'd decided to save them all, but she was only giving Logan three. All of him and his mom. There were a couple of his father at different ages, several of him and Logan's mom together, and one of the trio. She knew Logan wasn't in a mindset to be able to look at them now. But one day, he'd want them, and she'd know when it was time to let him know she'd kept them.

Now she sat in front of the hope chest. She was keeping everything in there, too. Old report cards. Book reports. His mother's diaries. A few letters his father had written to his mother to apologize for some bad days and nights over the years. She could imagine Everett Winston feeling terribly about the previous evening's strife that he'd caused and leaving a letter in an envelope with Connie's name across the front on the kitchen table. Connie had saved the letters. They were full of apologies and promises to do better, be better. Each one, several years apart, saying basically the same thing. They were hard to read after a while, and Annabel would save these but again not show them to Logan. Maybe not ever. She'd see.

There were a few things left in the hope chest. Another envelope and a few very old pieces of artwork from when Logan was in kindergarten. She turned over the envelope, surprised it was addressed to Logan. In Everett's handwriting. She wondered how it had gotten to the very bottom of the hope chest. Had Logan seen it and put it there? She doubted it or he'd have mentioned it. Maybe. Or maybe it had been on top of the pile in the chest when Michael had sorted through it and he'd put it back first. So it was at the bottom.

Maybe.

She almost felt like she shouldn't read it. There were no other letters from Logan's dad to him. Should she just give it to Logan unread?

No. He'd entrusted her with this job, and she'd read the letter and make the determination.

She took a breath and took the letter from the unsealed envelope.

Logan, I'm mad as hell at you but I want you to know I didn't mean what I said about being glad your mother is dead. I'm not. I also don't think you're a disappointment. I never did. I've always been proud of you, especially for somehow not ending up like me.

I see you're a big-time bull rider now. Your mother would be very proud.—Dad.

Annabel gasped again, her hand flying to her mouth. The letter was dated just a month before Everett Winston died. She read the letter again, tears falling down her cheeks. This would mean something to Logan. It might take him a while to internalize it, but it would have an effect. It would free him of the pain in his chest. She believed that.

She glanced at her phone—it was time to go back to the cabin to await Logan and Cody from their return from school. Today was their last full day together, and Logan had texted earlier, on his way to Cody's school for the show-and-tell about spending the afternoon, the three of them, exploring Clover Mountain, maybe having a picnic there.

Like old times, she'd thought when she'd gotten the text, remembering their picnic in the shallow cave almost eight years ago. The night, she was sure, Cody was conceived.

But now the idea of a second trip, a second picnic, felt sweet instead of bittersweet. She was going to let Logan go. She was going to be the mother Cody needed while both he and Logan found their footing in their new lives as father and son. Cody first. She'd had a good long talk with her mom after she'd returned to the ranch from her tour. Dinah thought that Annabel had the right attitude and that everything would work out, and she swore up and down that she wouldn't say it if she didn't believe it.

The letter would help Logan let go. Let him be who he wanted instead of living with those terrible words, that bullet in his heart. She'd show him the letter tonight. As her heartfelt goodbye to any hopes that the three of them could be a family.

A half hour later, as she waited for Logan to pick her up from the parking area at the ranch, a text pinged her phone.

Logan.

Cody called me Daddy as he walked down the hall from show-and-tell just now. First time. He'd added a heart emoticon with an arrow through it.

She almost texted back: That boy sure loves you. But deleted it. Then: That's so sweet, but that felt banal so she deleted it, too. She went with three red hearts.

And hit Send before she realized she should have sent just *two* hearts—for him and Cody. But she'd added herself in there, too.

Logan sat on the wide expanse of cliff on Clover Mountain overlooking a beautiful drop of evergreens and a creek, Cody between him and Annabel. They'd been hiking and exploring the caves for the past couple of hours, and all their stomachs were growling. Logan had stopped at a gourmet take-out on the way to pick up Annabel after the show-and-tell, also buying a backpack with a cooler bag in it to hold all the stuff. He'd let Cody choose the various sandwiches and fruits and treats and had thrown in a picnic blanket and three sun hats, which they all wore.

"Cody," Annabel said after taking a bite of her sandwich, "did you tell Logan my favorite sub of all time is chicken and pesto on a French baguette?"

Cody grinned. "Yup. I remembered the pesto part too even though I never remember what it *is*."

Annabel laughed. "It's a yummy sauce made from pine nuts."

Logan listened to the conversation, chowing down on his own sub, a turkey club. Cody was having a three-layer peanut butter and jelly sandwich. He would be content to sit here all day, talking about favorite foods, feeling the almost-summer breeze in his hair, watching the delight on his child's face. Looking at Annabel Dawson. That he could do forever.

Cody had already told his mom all about the show-and-tell, including his teacher telling two kids that they were asking nosy questions. Annabel had darted her gaze to him with concern but he'd shaken his head. The whole experience had been great. And Logan had to learn to expect these questions; he was a public figure in Wyoming and people felt that they could ask anything. He needed to have ready answers.

"Remember when Joel Fundy asked if you were

gonna stay in Bear Ridge or be a bull rider?" Cody said, taking a sip from his juice box.

Logan looked at Cody, a little surprised to see the hint of frown on the boy's face. He'd thought he'd handled that one well, that Cody was okay with the response. *I'll always come back. That's a promise.*

All of a sudden, tears slipped down Cody's cheeks. He shot a glance to Annabel, who looked like she might cry herself but he could see her squaring her shoulders to be strong for her son.

"Cody, I—" Logan began, determined to assure the boy he would be back, that he'd always come back.

But Cody had run off.

And within seconds, he was out of view.

"There are so many steep cliff drops," Annabel said, her voice full of worry. "Do you see him?" she asked, turning around in a circle, frantically looking.

Logan ran up ahead where there was a bit of a clearing. "Cody!" he called out. "Please come back. I love you and want to talk to you, son."

Silence. Just the breeze in the trees. And a woodpecker making a racket.

"Cody, honey," Annabel called out. "Just call out and we'll come to you, okay?"

More silence.

"I don't want Daddy to leave tomorrow," came the tearful voice. Then sobs.

Logan's legs wobbled. He and Annabel ran in the

direction of the voice and found Cody sitting under a tree, knees pulled up to the chest, arms around them tight, tears streaming.

Oh, Cody, Logan thought, his heart so heavy he expected to crash to his knees.

"Cody," Annabel said, rushing under the tree. She sat beside him and put her arm around him.

"I made a promise to you today, Cody. That I'll always come back. Always. We're going to make a schedule. I'll work on it when I get to my cabin after this and show it to your mom, okay?"

"So I'll always know when I'll see you?" Cody asked, wiping away his tears.

Logan should have realized how much reassuring Cody would need. One line wasn't going to cut it. He would have to constantly let the boy know he loved him, that he'd come see him and when and what time. And not be a second late.

Logan nodded. "Yes. You have my word."

Cody burrowed his head into his mother's chest and she put her arms around him, then he scrambled out and ran into Logan's arms.

I love you, he thought, closing his eyes as he wrapped his arms around his son. "I love you."

"I love you, too, Daddy," Cody said, looking up at him with those big hazel eyes.

"How about we head back to the cabin?" Annabel said, coming out from under the tree. He had the feeling she was very purposely looking everywhere but at Logan.

Some damage had been done.

Or maybe this was all part of figuring this out. How to make this work. The joint custody. When he got back to the cabin, he'd call his lawyer.

As they put their sandwich wrappers and bottles in the backpack and headed back down Clover Mountain, Logan tried to imagine what the scene would be like getting into Savannah's Range Rover tomorrow. Would Cody cling to him and tear out Logan's heart? Probably. And Logan was just going to have to deal.

This was going to be messy. There would be hard times and beautiful times. But he had to take days like today—a combination of both—and just straight-out rough days if he wanted the beautiful moments. Like in the hallway after show-and-tell. Like just now.

I love you, Daddy.

He would never forget both moments as long as he breathed.

Annabel sat on the edge of Cody's bed, watching his chest rise and fall. After his bath, he'd fallen asleep before she even got through saying the words *good night*. He was that tired. But it had been some day.

She heard the gentle tap on the door. Logan.

She pressed a light kiss to Cody's forehead, then

left the room, closing the door behind her, and went downstairs.

She took a deep breath as she opened the door. This was it. The last night together. He'd leave tomorrow morning, his manager coming to get him at 10:00 a.m. *You wanted platonic and you got it*, she thought ruefully.

He looked so handsome, so sexy, and she was so in love with him that she almost just grabbed him to her and kissed him. But she just said, "Come on in."

"Cody's asleep?" he asked, shutting the door.

She nodded, trying to keep herself together.

"I have a schedule," he said. "I called my lawyer when I got back—"

She froze for a moment. "Wait—you spoke to a lawyer? About the schedule?"

"Yeah, and now I have a draft of a possible joint custody agreement. It's very basic, just that we'll have fifty-fifty custody, Mother's Day with you, Father's Day with me, stuff like that. We'll each have Cody every other birthday. If we decide that's how we want it, I mean."

Annabel bristled—oh boy, did she—but she'd gotten to know this man so well that she couldn't even be angry. Or even worried—about what his likely five-hundred-bucks-an-hour lawyer had counseled him with and this draft custody agreement. He was clinging to "set in stone" for his and Cody's sakes. He needed something definitive so that he could leave with a clear heart and mind. She understood this.

"You can leave that with me," she said, gesturing at the document in his hands. "I'll look it over."

He set it on the coffee table. "I'd like to have Cody come to Blue Smoke next weekend when the *New York Times* reporter and videographer will be there. I'd like for him to be part of that."

"That's fine," she said. "I'd like to come with him, though. Until I'm used to you picking him up and taking him far away. I'll stay at a hotel in town, and Cody can stay with you, of course."

"You can both stay with me at my condo. I have two guest bedrooms."

She couldn't find her voice and so nodded, her chin feeling wobbly. She would eventually have to get used to letting Cody go solo with his father.

But as she looked at Logan, the veneer he'd come over with dropped off and the Logan she knew was back.

"I don't know how I'm going to say goodbye to him tomorrow," he said suddenly. "Or you," he added, his voice almost breaking.

"Let's sit down," she said, going over to the sofa. He sat beside her. Close enough that their thighs were touching. "I made a vow that I was going to let you go. No trying to keep you here. No using Cody as a means for an end to suit me—even if it would suit him, too. We will make this work. It's not ideal but your life is in Blue Smoke, on the road. You love Cody and I believe that. So I can let you go, Logan. We'll make this work," she repeated.

He turned slightly toward her, reaching out a hand to her cheek, but she moved over an inch.

She could *not* let him touch her or she'd lose it. She'd start sobbing. *Platonic, platonic, platonic.* "I have something for you," she said. "I found it while sorting through the things in the hope chest. It's an unsent letter from your father to you."

His face fell. "What? From my father?"

She nodded. "I almost didn't read it but I thought I'd better before giving it to you." She took it from her tote bag on the floor beside the coffee table and handed it to him.

He stared at it, turning it over in his hands. "I don't know, Annabel. I'm not sure I want to read it."

"You should," she said. "It's a good letter, Logan."

"Yeah?" he said, surprise lighting his handsome face.

She nodded. "Go back to your cabin and read it. I think you'll want privacy when you do."

He stared at the letter and then back at her. Then he gave her hand and a squeeze and stood up and left.

And Annabel flopped over on the sofa and cried.

Chapter Eighteen

Logan was glad it was too dark to read the letter on the way to his cabin. He held it, turning it over and looking at his father's handwriting. The envelope just said *Logan*.

When he arrived at his cabin, he went around back and turned on the patio light. He sat in his favorite chaise, the stars and moonlight illuminating the white envelope.

He stared at it, hard, and then finally took out the letter. It was dated just a month before Everett Winston died.

Logan swallowed and read it.

Logan, I'm mad as hell at you but I want you to know I didn't mean what I said about being glad your mother is dead. I'm not. I also don't think you're a

*disappointment. I never did. I've always been proud
of you, especially for somehow not ending up like me.
I see you're a big-time bull rider now. Your mother
would be very proud.—Dad.*

Tears pricked the backs of his eyes and he swiped
at them. *Dammit, Dad.* He'd spent so many years
holding on to his anger, his hurt. And just like that,
his father apologizes from the grave when he wasn't
ready for it, wasn't expecting it.

Clutching the letter, he went into the living room
and looked at the pile of photographs on the sofa.
Annabel must have sorted them. The Keep pile had
only three photos, facing up. The rest of the photos
were in an unmarked stack beside it. He turned over
the first one. Him, his mother and father when he
was seven. Cody's age. At the park in town, Logan
holding pieces of bread his mother had brought so
he could feed the ducks. His father's arm was around
his mother's shoulder.

He put the photo down, not ready for all this.

What he'd do instead was pack. On the way back
from Clover Mountain, Cody had asked if they could
all have breakfast together in the morning at his
cabin and asked his mom if they could have chocolate chip pancakes. Annabel had said sure.

Logan was expected there at seven, and then he'd
walk Cody down to meet the school bus at the gates.
He'd give his son a great big hug. Then he'd try his
best to focus on getting back to practicing, on the

competition, and go back to his own cabin and make sure he had all his stuff. At ten, Savannah was coming to pick him and Michael Finnegan up to head back to Blue Smoke.

He'd spoken to Michael before the show-and-tell today, and the guy was beside himself with excitement. Logan had heard Michael's voice crack when he said, "Really?" after Cody explained he'd spoken to his manager and she'd set up a job for him with the rodeo. When it came to knowing that was he was doing was right, he was sure only about this part.

Everything else was heart-wrenching. The thought of leaving made him feel like hell.

But staying meant...

What? What did it mean? That he'd give up defending his title? The title he'd had for three years running? To earn more medals? More money? More spokesperson gigs?

When he had a son who'd said *I love you, Daddy,* twice today and meant it?

He stared at the letter he clutched in his hand. He didn't need to read it again. He knew what it said. He appreciated the letter, but he wasn't ready to forgive his father. That would probably take a little time.

What he needed was Annabel and Cody to help him get there.

"Is he here yet?" Cody asked the next morning, his footsteps pounding down the stairs of the cabin.

Annabel was in the kitchen, mixing the pancake batter, which smelled heavenly. "It's about twenty-five minutes too early," she called.

She was hoping her eyes weren't too red-rimmed from the crying she'd done last night.

And just five minutes ago. Knowing Cody was going to wake up any minute. Knowing Logan was coming to say goodbye.

Knowing that their second chance had come and gone, but grateful that he was committed to Cody.

"Oh," he said, the footsteps slower as she came into the kitchen. He eyed the bag of chocolate chips next to the tissues. "Yay, I can't wait for chocolate chip pancakes!"

Oh, Cody, she thought, kneeling down to wrap her boy in a hug.

"But boo that Daddy is leaving this morning. I know he's coming back, though."

She nodded firmly. "He definitely will be back." How she'd get through it was another story, though.

A knock came at the door. She glanced at her phone on the counter, next to the box of tissues she'd half used up on her tears. It was only six thirty-five. She frowned, wondering who it was. Logan wouldn't be a half hour early, would he?

Cody ran to the door. "Who is it, please?"

"It's Daddy," came Logan's voice.

Annabel came out to the entryway. Cody flung open the door and there Logan was.

"You came extra early, yay!" Cody said. "Now we have longer before you have to leave."

Logan kneeled down. "I'm not leaving, Cody. I'm going to stay here. Forever. Just like your seventh birthday wish asked me to."

Cody's eyes widened. So did Annabel's. "But Savannah is coming to get you at ten o'clock," Cody said. "You're going back to Blue Smoke."

Logan shook his head. "Nope. I'm staying right here in Bear Ridge. Where my son is. And where his mother is—the woman I love with all my heart."

Annabel gasped.

Cody gasped.

He stood up and walked over to Annabel, taking both her hands. "I've loved you since the first day I met you. I thought I had to prove something to my father, but what I realized last night after reading that letter you found is that all this time, I was trying to prove something to *myself.* And nothing was ever good enough."

"I'm not really understanding this," Cody said earnestly.

Annabel's eyes teared up, but happy tears this time.

Logan knelt down in front of Cody again. "You, Cody. You love your daddy. So I must be doing something right."

"I do love you," Cody said. "And not just because you're my hero. But because you're you."

Logan pulled Cody to him. Annabel swiped at her cheeks.

He lifted Cody in his arms. "I'm finally allowed to do this," he said, upping his chin at his wrist. He walked over to Annabel and put his arm around her. "We're a family. And I'd like to be your husband, if you'll have me."

Annabel's heart couldn't take much more happiness. "I love you, Logan. And yes, I'll marry you."

"Yay, we're a family!" Cody exclaimed. "Can we have the chocolate chip pancakes now?"

Annabel and Logan both laughed and they walked into the kitchen, each holding one of Cody's hands.

"We're a family," Logan agreed with a nod. "I'll bring Michael down to meet Savannah at the gate at ten. But I'll be walking back right here—and staying put."

"How will Savannah take the news that you're giving up bull riding?" Annabel asked as she turned on a burner under the griddle. Ready to make pancakes for her family.

My family.

"Oh, I think she'll be happy for me," Logan said. "For *all* of us. Plus, she'll have a new project—helping Michael find his way in rodeo and make a fresh start."

A fresh start. Annabel loved the sound of that. Today truly felt like the first day of forever.

* * * * *

#2995 A MAVERICK REBORN
Montana Mavericks: Lassoing Love • by Melissa Senate

Handsome loner cowboy Bobby Stone has his issues—from faking his own death three years ago to discovering a twin brother he never knew. But headstrong rodeo queen Tori Hawkins is just the woman to break through his tough facade. First with a rambunctious fling...and later with the healing love Bobby's always needed...

#2996 RANCHER TO THE RESCUE
Men of the West • by Stella Bagwell

Mack Barlow may have broken Dr. Grace Hollister's heart in high school, but sparks still fly when the now-single father walks into her medical clinic. His young daughter is adorable. And he's...too dang sexy by far! Can a very busy divorced mom take a second chance on loving the man who once left her behind?

#2997 OLD DOGS, NEW TRUTHS
Sierra's Web • by Tara Taylor Quinn

When heiress Lindsay Warren-Smythe assumes a false identity to meet her biological father, she's not expecting to develop a connection with her new coworker, Cole Bennet, and his lovable dog. Cole has learned the hard way not to trust beautiful liars with his heart, so when he lets his guard down with Lindsay, will her lies tear them apart?

#2998 MATCHMAKER ON THE RANCH
Forever, Texas • by Marie Ferrarella

Rancher Chris Parnell has known Rosemary Robinson all his life. But working side by side with the beautiful vet to diagnose the sickness affecting his cattle kicks him completely out of his friend zone! Roe can't deny the attraction sizzling between them. But will her friend with benefits stick around once the cattle mystery is solved?

#2999 HER YOUNGER MAN
Sutton's Place • by Shannon Stacey

Widow Laura Thompson falling for a younger man? Not on your life! Except Riley Thompson is so dang charming. And handsome. And everything Laura's missing in her life. The town seems to be against their romance. Including Riley's boss...who's Laura's son! Are Riley and Laura strong enough to take a stand for love?

#3000 IN TOO DEEP
Love at Hideaway Wharf • by Laurel Greer

Chef Kellan Murphy is determined to fulfill his sister's dying wish. But placing an ocean-fearing man in a scuba diving class is ridiculous! Instructor Sam Walker can't resist helping the handsome wannabe diver overcome his fears. And their unexpected connection is the perfect remedy for Sam's own hidden pain...

**YOU CAN FIND MORE INFORMATION ON UPCOMING HARLEQUIN TITLES,
FREE EXCERPTS AND MORE AT HARLEQUIN.COM.**

HSECNM0623

Get 3 FREE REWARDS!

We'll send you 2 FREE Books plus a FREE Mystery Gift.

FREE Value Over **$20**

Both the **Harlequin® Special Edition** and **Harlequin® Heartwarming™** series feature compelling novels filled with stories of love and strength where the bonds of friendship, family and community unite.